Sarah Dana Greenough

Lilian

Sarah Dana Greenough

Lilian

ISBN/EAN: 9783337007515

Printed in Europe, USA, Canada, Australia, Japan

Cover: Foto ©Andreas Hilbeck / pixelio.de

More available books at **www.hansebooks.com**

LILIAN.

BOSTON:
TICKNOR AND FIELDS.
1863.

Entered according to Act of Congress, in the year 1863,
By TICKNOR AND FIELDS,
in the Clerk's Office of the District Court of the District of Massachusetts.

RIVERSIDE, CAMBRIDGE:
STEREOTYPED AND PRINTED BY H. O. HOUGHTON.

LILIAN.

I.

An open glade. In the midst an old oak-tree. At its foot a girl, reading. The landscape sweet, tender, full of peace. The girl's face sad, shadowy, full of unrest.

She sits reading the Prologue to "Faust." She grasps the forbidden fruit. Shall no hand stay her ere she have tasted of it, and the knowledge of Good and Evil have closed the gates of Childhood's Paradise behind her forever?

Who was this girl, and how came she to be sitting under the old oak-tree, reading "Faust"?

To answer these questions, we must row back, far up the fast swelling river of Lilian's life, till we reach the brooklet of her seventh year.

Her parents lie in the quiet graveyard of the gray little church below the hill. Had you questioned of the parish register, "How long

since ? " it would have replied, " Two years."
Had you asked of little Lilian's heart, it would
have answered, " Yesterday."

She had mourned them with a passionate
grief, beyond her childish years. No second
attachment came to loosen the tenacious clasp
with which, as ivy· around a fallen tree, her
affections clung to their memory. Caressed
and indulged though she was, the child instinctively felt that all who rightly loved and
comprehended her had passed from her sight
forever. Month by month, the void of their
absence grew blacker and wider. As her com-
plex nature began to unfold, she felt the more
deeply the need of that lost love to harmonize
what was discordant within her, to solve the rid-
dles, to clear up the enigmas of her youthful
life, with its sweet wisdom to reconcile her with
herself.

Will and Ideality she had inherited from her
father, Impulsiveness and Sensitiveness from her
mother. Had they lived, her parents would
have understood the child, — bone of their bone,
flesh of their flesh, spirit of their spirit, — her
father through his intellect, her mother through
her heart. But they were not. The image of

her graceful, sweet-voiced, dark-eyed mother, —
the remembrance of the gay smile, the flashing
blue eyes, the caressing tones of her father, —
were all that remained of them to Lilian. To
whom now was she to bring her yearnings, her
questionings, her fears, her delights? To whom
impart the ecstasy that thrilled through her from
all that was beautiful: the sunlight, the flowers,
the music of the birds; and to whom whisper
her creeping dread of all ugly and harmful
things? To whom reveal the keen desire that at
times possessed her to run away to the woods
and live in freedom with the birds and the
squirrels; and to whom repeat the song that she
heard the rivulet sing from under its grassy
banks to the little tender moon that stayed up
all the morning to listen? To whom recount
the lament of the night wind, repenting in vain
remorse of its wicked deeds upon the sea; and
to whom describe the wild chase of monstrous,
threatening forms across the cloudy sky? To
whom confide her longings for a happiness she
dreamed, but knew not; and to whom bring the
questionings that vaguely stirred within her of
this world and the next? To none; for little
Lilian, the pet and darling of the household,

daintily tended, tenderly cherished, had no one to understand her inmost wants, no one to love. To love as she was capable of loving; not as she loved her grandmother, one vast, soft cushion, body and mind, and her tall Irish staghound, Great Heart; — beings who might be considered to stand nearly upon a level as to intellect, although the dog possessed one incontestable advantage, in that, as he never spoke, no one could find out the full extent of his limitations. Not as she loved solemn Jonathan, the old coachman, who had given her first lessons in riding, slowly pacing round the stable yard, holding her on the slippery back of one of his stalwart, iron-gray coach horses; and who later, with the long-winded perseverance of an English fox-hunter, scoured the country for thirty miles round after her snorting, glossy black mare. Not as she loved round, rosy Peter, the man-servant, who had from her earliest childhood, improvised for her irregular feasts at all sorts of irregular hours, abducting the sunniest peaches and rarest nectarines from the trellised fruit garden, and secreting the choicest treasures of the pantry for her sole use and benefit. Not as she loved trig, black-eyed Becky, the maid,

who never ended her daily task of braiding and
coiling the unending length of her young mistress's silky hair, without exclaiming in a tone,
half laudatory, half self-gratulatory, " Well, now,
Miss Lilian, you do look most beautiful ! " Not
as she loved pale, methodistical Sophy, the cook,
who had. uncomplainingly given up her sunny
back-kitchen parlor to the uses of an aviary, and
who resignedly saw the hours once set aside for
the study of the Bible and of Baxter's " Saint's
Rest " sacrificed to the daily encroaching claims
of Lilian's canaries. Yet she loved them all
well, better than in strictest justice they de-
served; for all had, ever since her birth, done
their utmost to spoil her. Such persevering and
consistent endeavor could not fail to meet with
some reward. Lilian was more than a little
spoiled. Not in the vulgar acceptation of the
term. No petty, provoking faults sullied the
sweet life of the lovely, caressing child, but an
untamed energy of will, an unchecked intensity
of impulse were slowly and silently evolving
themselves ; — destructive, electric forces, yet hid
within the sunny heaven of little Lilian's smile.

II.

ONCE and once only during her petted childhood did the latent vehemence of Lilian's nature
break forth in full force, exploding as suddenly,
and well-nigh as murderously as a bombshell.

High among the strange, barbaric weapons
which lined the hall of the old mansion house,
relics of an outlandish taste of her great-grand-
father's, hung an Indian bow and quiver of
arrows. These, Lilian, fired by the example of
Robinson Crusoe, appropriated, and with charac-
teristic, most unchildlike perseverance, practised
with them until her hand and eye would have
done honor to her hero himself. Her weapons
were for the time her inseparable companions.

It chanced that, thus equipped, she was climbing one afternoon, high among the spreading
branches of the great tree at the bottom of the
garden, examining whether, should the house
happen to burn down in the night, and the
neighbors refuse to take her in, she could find
a place among the boughs· to sleep in like Robinson Crusoe, — a place where she could be
sure of not falling down and breaking her leg.
While thus busily engaged, her ear was smitten

by a woful sound. The piteous moaning of a kitten rose from the path, on the outer side of the garden-wall. Clambering along the overhanging branches, with anger and apprehension indescribable, she saw below her own pretty little kitten, swinging by its tail from the hand of an Italian organ-grinding boy.

"You wicked boy, put down my kitten; put her down this minute!" shrieked Lilian.

The boy looked up, grinning maliciously, with the habitual insolence of foreign vagrants in America; and turning, so as to face the child, began to swing the screaming kitten with redoubled energy, obviously intending, so soon as the momentum should be satisfactory, to launch it, head foremost, against the stone wall.

Not an instant was to be lost. White with rage, Lilian dropped astride on the great bough. The bow was strong, the arrow sharp, the arm of the little archer steady, the distance short. The bowstring twanged, and the whizzing arrow planted its lesson of humanity deep in the leg of the little brown Caligula, who fell to the ground with piercing shrieks. The kitten, suddenly released, disappeared with celerity; Lilian slipped down from the bough and stood over her prostrate foe, wringing her hands in pale and wild dismay, while the startled Great Heart from the inner side of the high garden-wall, Cerberus-like, barked, whined, and howled, all at once.

It is doubtful whether Lilian had ever, in the whole course of her life, heard of such a thing as Providential Interference; but certain it is that she devoutly believed in it from that moment when, in her direst extremity of need, a tall shadow fell across the yelling heap at her feet, and a deep voice of kindly tone said, in foreign accents to the wounded boy, —

" Cosa hai, poverello ? "

A lofty form stooped over the little Italian, whose cries ceased as by magic at the first sound of his native tongue. Gently and skilfully the arrow was extracted, the leg bound up with Lilian's pocket-handkerchief, and the little vagabond dismissed with a gratuity of silver coins, which brought a quick succession of glittering smiles over his dirty, tear-smeared face.

Still Lilian stood as if rooted to the ground, sobbing and speechless, till the gentleman, taking her hand, attempted to soothe her. " After all, the wound was but a slight one, and she had not intended to hurt the little boy." She snatched away her hand and chokingly exclaimed, —

" But I *did* do it on purpose. He was going to kill my kitten, and I tried to kill him first." And ere the stranger had recovered from his surprise at this new view of the case, the sobs died into gasps, and with a sickening groan the child reeled backward.

No cold, unyielding ground received her. The sinking little frame was lifted in strong arms, and the stranger, seating himself on the low, grassy bank, laid her head on his broad chest, and gently dried her pale, wet cheeks.

With still approach a sense of peace and protection ineffable stole over her. Slowly a soft, white cloud seemed to descend upon her and fold her into dream-land. The events of the past hour appeared to belong to another life. Her anger, her terror, her distress, had passed away. A pulseless quiet drowned her every sense; nor did she awake to the full consciousness of what had occurred, until she had been carried into the house and delivered into her grandmother's wondering arms.

Secretive, like all sensitive children, Lilian shunned all converse and comment upon her accident, as this outbreak of passion was termed by the partial household; but none the less firmly did she cherish in her inmost heart the conviction that the tall, strange gentleman had been divinely sent to save the organ-boy's life, — for with the imaginative ignorance of childhood she shiveringly believed that her anger had compromised the little Italian's existence, — and to preserve herself from the pains and penalties, earthly and eternal, attached to the crime of murder.

So that night and every night, after Becky, with loving words and energetic kisses, had deposited her darling in the smooth-spread solitude of the great white bed, where she lay like a blush rose-bud peeping from a snow-drift, and with parting benediction had closed the heavy door, Lilian, creeping from her covert and sliding down the slippery height, knelt in the shadowy stillness and completed the unfinished prayer begun at Becky's knee, devoutly thanking God for having sent the strange gentleman to help her when she had been so wicked, and penitently imploring that He would never, never let her be such a naughty girl again; then clambering up the old carved mahogany bedpost, like a kitten, she would slip into her yet warm nest and fall asleep, — the deep-toned voice and the grave, kindly eyes of the stranger mingling with her dreams.

III.

It might have been a fortnight later, when, with bent head and folded arms, a tall form was slowly pacing the road which skirted the churchyard wall. A lullaby, sung low in a childish voice, floated towards him on the still air. It came from the churchyard. The high wall shut out all view from the road, but turning an angle where it was lower, he saw within.

The setting sun shot long, level, golden bars athwart the dark trunks of the encircling trees, over a woful waste. Nature ran fierce riot, unreproved, over the deserted graves; and in sullen exultation, seemed to triumph over her fallen competitor, — Man.

From amid the writhing witch-grass, sharp-pointed nettles reared their purple heads, and white mulleins stretched rankly forth their tall, knotted, colorless spires. Giant dock-weeds spread wide their unwholesome leaves, as if to hide the sunken head-stones. Toadstools and mushrooms crouched livid on the dank mould, while across the untrodden path, snarling briers and poisonous creepers stretched their repellant arms, waving back the rare intruder on their assured domain.

No kindly remembrance, no loving, lingering care, extended its protection over the silent dwellers beneath. All lay unheeded, all were forgotten, save by one mourner, — one little child.

In the dark shadow of the wall, between two long, green, carefully tended graves, like a little white monumental effigy, sat Lilian, her great stag-hound crouching at her feet. The lullaby ceased, but she still sat motionless. The dog raised his head warily with a low growl, as the stranger, entering this home of desolation, approached her graves. Then she arose, and moving towards him, —

"Come away," she said jealously.

He followed as she led the way out of the graveyard, and walked beside her along the path, thinking she was the strangest, prettiest little creature he had ever seen. The fancy seized him to make her talk.

"What is your name, little one?"

"Lilian."

Rather thinking aloud than calculating the effect of his words, the stranger continued, —

"Are you lonely?"

"No."

A pause. The living pain buried in Lilian's

heart turned restlessly. The erect head drooped, and in a changed voice she answered again, —

" Yes, very."

" Poor child; I have pained her," thought the stranger.

They were passing the church-porch. " Will you come and sit with me in the porch, Lilian ? " he said, in the deep, pleasant voice she remembered so well. " It is not the first time we have sat together, you know."

The shadow on Lilian's forehead passed. She looked up with a coy, trusting smile, and turned towards the porch. He took her on his knee and sat for a while silently smoothing her silky hair. Lilian scarcely breathed; — she was in a trance of happiness. He who mingled with her daily and nightly dreams was actually holding her again upon his knee. Would he speak once more to her ? What would he say ? At length the question came.

" Do you often come here, my child ? "

There was an indescribable compassion in the tone, that opened Lilian's heart. She felt impelled to tell this stranger, whom she had seen only once before in her life, things that she had never dreamed of saying to her grandmother, nor to Becky, nor to any one else. Full and free came her answers, certain of comprehension, sure of sympathy.

"Yes, very often. I love to come here."

"And you sing in the churchyard?"

"Yes. My mother used to sing me to sleep with that song, and my father used to sit holding her hand and listening. I come with Great Heart very often, — Great Heart was my father's dog, — and sing it to them. I know they like to hear it."

The stranger pressed a silent kiss upon little Lilian's forehead.

She began to question in her turn.

"Have you got any father or mother?"

"No."

"Any brothers or sisters?"

"No."

"Any grandmamma to take care of you?"

"No."

"What's your name?"

"Clinton."

"Where do you live?"

"In the house just above us?"

"What, have you come to live in the great house on the hill?"

"Yes."

"I'm glad. Now I must go home. — Good-by."

"Will you give me a kiss, Lilian?" said the stranger, ere he put her down.

The cherub head was thrown back, the little rosy arms cast frankly around his neck, the sweet lips pressed to his dark cheek. Then, followed by the great hound, the child flitted into the fading sunlight and disappeared.

——◆——

IV.

DWELLING in the comparative solitude of the country, not far apart, Lilian and Mr. Clinton often met. One of those rare and beautiful attachments which we sometimes see existing in spite of, perhaps because of, the widest differences in age and character, sprang up between the studious, stately gentleman, and the little impulsive child; devoted and enthusiastic on her part, tranquil but tender on his.

Grandmamma, "who had always known Mr. Clinton's family," looked with complacency upon the growing intimacy. "Lilian," she said, "had never seen much of other children, and those she had seen she had not seemed to like. The child needed some sort of a companion, and since she

had taken such an extraordinary fancy to Mr.
Clinton, and he seemed to like to have her with
him, for her part she was glad to know her in
such good hands, safe and out of harm's way."

Now came happy days to little Lilian. Her
heart and intellect expanded like flowers in sunlight. Each moment fell like a golden drop into
the crystal cup of her young life. She was
loved. Her beauty fascinated Mr. Clinton's eye,
her affection touched his heart, her delicate nature with its core of fire interested his imagination, her sunny presence shed pleasant light
through his home. Often did he look up from
his book or his writing to meet the loving gaze
bent upon him from the clear eyes of the child,
standing noiselessly at the half-opened door, pa-
tiently awaiting his summons. Then, wonted
welcome given, she would draw a cushion to his
feet, and place herself there, leaning her glossy
head against his knee, motionless with happiness.

The delight of those silent hours; the library
with its sober, many-tinted lining of awe-inspir-
ing tomes, half darkened to exclude the summer
heat; the rare old pictures, the marble busts, the
soft low hum of insect life without; the hush of

cool stillness within, only broken by the turning of a leaf or the motion of the pen; — would Lilian ever be so happy again?

She loved Mr. Clinton with a religious adoration. He was so great, so good, so glorious! If she could only do something to show him how much she loved him! As she sat hour after hour at his feet, she would imagine wild scenes in which in fancy her affection would at length have scope. He would be bound by savages, and she, in the creeping silence of the night, lighted by the red glare of the embers of the fire, would steal across the sleeping forms of the fierce, red-skinned blood-hounds, and cut his bonds; then lead him to where she had tied two horses, and they would mount and be far away ere day should break, and the grim Indians miss their prey.

Or his house would take fire in the night, and the black smoke would be pouring from all the windows, and the open portal would show a fiery glare within, with serpent-like flames springing from every door; and he would be in his room asleep, and no one would dare to go in to wake him; and she would throw a blanket over her, and rush through the smoke and past the flames, and reach his door, and rouse him, just in time to

save him, before the stairs fell in. Or (this was
the worst of all, and always brought a groan),
they would be walking together in the woods, and
he would grow tired, and lie down under a great,
dark tree, and fall asleep, and she would sit down
and watch him, and, while watching him, would
hear a rustling in the tree above, and look up and
see the fiery eyes of a great panther fixed upon
him, and then she would softly run forward and
stand under the panther, and it would spring down
upon her, and eat her up; then, being no longer
hungry, it would go away, and not hurt Mr.
Clinton. Wild fancies all, but containing a germ
of truth. Lilian was capable of exposing, nay, of
sacrificing her life itself, for those she loved.

But at length the book or letters would be laid
aside, and Mr. Clinton, lifting her on his knee,
would talk with her, and tell her of wonderful
things, — of the lofty halls of the Mammoth Cave,
with their mirrors, pillars, and curtains of glittering stalactites, its black river, filled with eyeless
fishes, its mysterious passages, stretching miles
and miles away, so deep into the earth that travellers have come back after many days unable to
reach the end, — its Indian princess, whom the first
discoverers found, decked with savage ornaments,

seated in funereal state, in the great rocky arm-chair of one of the shining halls, — of the mounds and breastworks, imaging serpents, and strange Eastern symbols found in the far West, left by vanished races, — of the great Salt Desert, which spreads like a frozen sea, gleaming as far as the eye can reach, strewn with the bones of man and beast, — of rough-clad miners, digging the heavy quartz from the wild gorges of Californian mountains, and crushing it with ponderous hammers, to extract the shining gold. Of marvels of the West and of the East (and of such of Nature's hidden laws her occult forces and secret processes as a child might understand) he taught her, listening with suspended breath ; and, when the new knowledge had been curiously examined, wondered at, and stored away, Lilian would nestle closer to him, and whisper, —

" Now is the time you tell me about God."

———◆———

V.

GLAD as the sunlight, joyous as the rainbow, so brilliant, so evanescent, was Lilian's summer dream. Must in this world even a little child learn that to love is to suffer !

Slowly Lilian walked up the garden-walk. She seated herself in the shade under the drawing-room windows. The sound of voices from within came upon her ear, but came unheeded. She sat looking through the tree-tops up into the sky, watching the little white clouds as they dissolved in the fervent blue, and musing wistfully. Mr. Clinton had bidden her good-by, for an absence of a few days, with a promise to come and see her as soon as he returned. It was a whole fortnight ago, and yet he had not come. She missed him so much. When should she see him again? Suddenly her attention was arrested by the concluding words of a sentence, spoken in a louder key than those which had preceded it.

"—— so very ill!"

"Yes," answered her grandmother's voice, "the doctor says it is a bad case."

" And poor, little Lilian, she's so fond of him; how does she take it?"

" Oh, we don't let her know anything about it. She'd fret her life out."

Lilian's heart gave a fearful leap, then stood still. There was a rushing sound in her ears. For a moment, she saw nothing. Then, she knew not how, she found herself speeding along the road, a horrible fear clutching at her throat. On — on — through the scorching heat, — on — on. She shuddered, as though an icy wind had struck on her, as she passed under the twilight of the churchyard trees. Was *he*, too, on his way thither? The great house rose before her, on the hill, — nearer — nearer. She was there. She crept stealthily along the silent hall. There was a strange hush in the house. Past the drawing-rooms, past the library, through his dressing-room, she stood at his open door, the blood surging in heavy waves through breast and brain. There was a stillness like the shadow of death within. As she gazed with eyes whose longing look seemed almost able to pierce the heavy curtains that shrouded what she loved best on earth from her sight, she heard a slight stir as if a head turned upon a pillow, — one faint word, —

" Water."

There was no response. On tiptoe she advanced, and stole a cautious glance around the room. In the farthest corner, sat a woman she had never seen before, sleeping. With a pang of joy, the child glided forward, took the cup of cold water from its stand, and held it to those beloved lips, but shivered as she saw those wasted features, and

that blue, wan hue. He drank, and was refreshed.
He looked on her, and knew her. Too weak for
words, he would have raised his hand as in the
old caress. The silken head bent low to meet it,
but in vain. Wearily it fell back. With a woman's fortitude, Lilian pressed back her tears.
She smiled bravely as she took the hot, nerveless
hand in her fresh, soft palms, and looked into his
face with love unutterable.

A healing influence seemed to flow from out the
child. Her touch sent grateful coolness through
the fevered frame. That loving gaze gave to the
weary, wandering thought something whereon to
rest. His look fixed on hers, his hand clasped in
hers, Mr. Clinton fell into a quiet slumber, the
first for many days.

Lilian, statue still, watched and prayed, — prayed as a little child prays, with a vague, uncertain
hope that God would see how wretched she was,
and hear her.

The slow hours drew on. The breath of the
sick man came in fuller, deeper inspirations, the
burning palm insensibly grew moist, the contracted
brow relaxed. Still he slept on.

The nurse awoke, and saw her place thus filled.
She advanced in ruffled dignity of office to re-

monstrate; but, ere she had breathed the first word of her protest, was waved back; so fierce a light flashing from the child's eyes, that she silently returned to her treacherous easy-chair, there to await the doctor's decree of expulsion against the daring intruder.

The shadows lengthened, widened, and blended. The air grew cool with dew; the evening song of the crickets came through the gathering gloom, ere the sick man wakened. He looked at her long and earnestly. He pressed the hand that claspingly held his. He spoke. All her senses centred in her ear.

"Dear child."

Her throat swelled. She *must* ask him.

"Are you better?"

"Yes."

Awe came upon her, greater even than her joy. Had God really heard her prayer? Had he, at her cry, bent down from his throne, and, clement, taken pity on her misery, changed his dread decree, and given Life for Death?

"Miss Lilian," whispered a voice from the door.

Lilian cast a rapid glance at the half-hidden speaker. The moment of the expected encounter had come. Releasing the hand she still held, she entered the dressing-room, and softly closed the door. Pale, erect, and fiery, she faced the quailing Becky.

"Becky, don't speak. I know all you've got to say. Now do you listen, and then do you go back, and tell grandmamma every word you hear. I *won't* go home. I mean to stay here, and take care of Mr. Clinton. He wants me, and I shall stay. I shall take care of him till he gets well; and if he does not get well," — here her voice almost choked, but with a powerful effort the child again commanded it, — " if he dies, I mean to die too. — Good-by, Becky."

She threw her arms around Becky's neck, kissed her, and disappeared in Mr. Clinton's room.

Slowly the astounded Becky retraced her steps, and punctually did she repeat to Lilian's grandmother the message she was charged to bear.

" She was all white, ma'am," Becky concluded her narration, " and she looked twice as tall as she ever did before, and her eyes shone like a cat's in the dark. She looked so like her father, when he was angry, that I was e'en a'most scared to see her. I think, ma'am, you'd better just let her be. No good never came of crossing her father; and it's my private 'pinion that no good 'll ever come of crossing Miss Lilian, neither."

Distressed as Mrs. DeKahn was at the ill success of her messenger, she was too entirely of Becky's opinion as to the hopelessness of any attempt at changing Lilian's determination, to make any further efforts; so she "gave up the point," as she expressed it, and contented herself with the most careful supervision of the child's toilet practicable at a distance.

When the little, round, fat, good-natured doctor, a fast friend of Lilian's, made his evening call, he found a notable change for the better in his patient; and being a man so wise in his generation as to entertain a profound conviction that Nature has many mysteries yet to be probed, and to firmly believe in the power and efficacy of Moral Medicine; he gave cheerful permission that the child should remain. But not without conditions. His professional visit over, he drew Lilian to the veranda, and with unprofessional directness began, —

"Now, my little girl, Mr. Clinton is better, and, what's more, I think you have had some-

thing to do with it. But don't let me have any
more standing up all the afternoon. You may
sit by him and hold his hand all day long if
you like, but don't stand, don't do anything to
fatigue yourself. If you get tired, it will be the
worse for him. And mind, you must go to bed
at the same hour that you do at home, and take
your meals regularly; and every day, after I
make my morning-call, I shall take you down
to see your grandmother, on my way to the vil-
lage, and you can run back with Great Heart.
Good-night. You're a good little girl, and I'd
much rather trust you to take care of him, than
that nurse."

So Lilian, full of thankfulness, pride, and happiness, was authoritatively installed at Mr. Clinton's bedside; and the fat little doctor, mounting
his gray horse, jogged through the twilight down
the road, mentally soliloquizing in a fragmentary,
jerking sort of way.

" Never could understand why holding a patient's hand reduces fever, and puts him to sleep.
But it does, — that's certain. Good child that,
— handy and reasonable. — Image of her mother!
— He's fond of her. — See that by the way he
looks at her. — Needs something about him that

he loves, — all patients do. — Feel better about him this evening. — Great thing that sleep! — Didn't like his looks at noon. — Ugly things these fevers. — But I think he'll get through."

With a feeling of inexpressible relief, Mr. Clinton on the morrow, saw the nurse, a ponderous, jelly-like woman, retreat to her newly assigned post in the dressing-room. His strong nerves had become morbidly sensitive, his rigidly controlled fancy, intolerably capricious. The presence of the woman had grown hateful to him. Her shapeless figure disgusted him, her elephantine tread oppressed him, her wheedling voice irritated him. The pillow smoothed by her toad-like hands felt uneasy to his head, the beverage they presented was nauseous to his taste. With all the strength his fever had left him, he had struggled against this aversion, but in vain. Day by day it increased upon him. Fanciful as a woman, unreasonable as a child, he shuddered whenever she approached him.

Now that she was gone out of his sight, the room seemed to grow larger, the air freer, and with a sigh of grateful relief he turned his eyes upon the dainty little guardian sitting by his side.

The air came fresh with morning odors through the open window. Little birds twittered from the garden walks. Soft clouds chased each other over the blue sky. A gentle wind stirred the tree-tops and waved the wreaths of honeysuckle that climbed around the casement. The glad and quiet content of all things without spread itself through the sick man's chamber. The tide of returning life stirred within him. He breathed deeply of the flower-scented air. He smiled as a little brown sparrow perched upon the window-sill, turning its restless head from side to side, with bright, quick eyes, curiously spying within. He watched the honeysuckle waving around the window, and then its shadow moving in concert on the floor. Little things pleased him. A still sense of happiness stole over him like a benediction. He felt that it was good to live.

Pleasant were those quiet, intensely vivid, yet dream-like days of convalescence. All the lighter duties of attendance Lilian assumed, and discharged with watchful, unassuming tact. She never asked a question, yet knew as by instinct when the pillow grew hard beneath the aching head, when the weary eyes coveted soft shadow, when the fevered lips craved the refreshing draught. Noiselessly she moved about the room on her ministrations, while Mr. Clinton's eyes with languid pleasure followed the music of her wavelike motion; or as she sat tranquilly vigilant before him, would scan her beauty with ever new delight; — her cloudy hair, her pure forehead, her creamy complexion, the delicate tracing of her features. Nought about the child was coarse, blurred, or ill-defined. She was finished like an antique gem.

As she would sit, in her light draperies of tinted muslin, on a low seat beside his bed, holding his hand hour after hour, — or, her lap filled with freshly-gathered flowers, fashioning wreaths and bouquets to gladden his sick room, her eyes lifted every little while with a silent, loving smile towards him, — Mr. Clinton could feel the very tendrils of his heart weaving themselves about her. He had always loved her, but now she grew infinitely dear to him. He felt towards her the tenderness of a father, the pride of a brother, the reverence of a man.

Beautiful was the love between them. Strange the reversal of their respective positions, — the child watching over the man.

No hand save hers might spread the snowy
napkin on the silver waiter, deck it with flowers,
and arrange the dainty meal to tempt the sick
man's taste. No touch save hers bathe his forehead with fragrant waters, and smooth back the
heavy masses of his hair. No arm but hers wave,
to cool the sultry air, the great Indian fan, gay
with peacock's feathers, stiff·with its huge crimson rosette. And later, when he could leave his
bed and lie on the sofa under the shadow of the
leafy-screened veranda, no voice save hers read
to him hour after hour his favorite books.

No relapse came to retard Mr. Clinton's re-
covery. ·A constitution that had never been tam-
pered with stood him in good stead. Erelong
his wonted strength returned, and he stood forth
again, vigorous as if the wing of Death had never
waved over him.

Lilian's watch was over. Her home with impatient voice demanded her. She must return.
And she returned, and all things were as they
were before, save that a tone of unconscious respect deepened the affection around her, and that
her grandmother from that time forward frequently declared that Lilian was so unlike other

children that it frightened her.—She was afraid the child was too good to live.

Little Lilian, with the fiery vehemence hiding in the deep places of her heart,—like a mine of gunpowder under a flowery bank,—too good to live!

Take courage, grandmamma. A very human little child it is. No angel at all.

———◆———

VI.

"You will find Lilian in the garden." Mr. Clinton came down the steps of the pillared porch into the great, old-fashioned garden. It was a pleasant place. The high stone wall that closed it in was hidden from view by a belt of heavy firs and light forest-trees, among whose branches the birds sang, and the little red squirrels frisked in all the security of their native woods. Tall Norway pines and graceful hemlocks, trailing their sweeping branches on the smooth green sod, towered from the broad terraces; while here and there the mountain laurel with its white, ruby-touched clusters, the rosy flush of the flowering almond, and the delicate, snowy blossoms of the fragrant syringa, perfumed the air.

Descending the stone steps of the terraces, he passed the sunny espaliers thick hung with crimson peaches, purple nectarines, and golden pears, where from overarching trellises the waving garlands of the luxuriant vines turned their silver linings to the sunset breeze.

Turning an angle formed by an advancing clump of pines, he came upon the painted statue of the red Indian, springing forth from his ambush in act to strike; grim and terrible to childish eyes, and startling even to their elders, meeting him unawares; and entered the flower-garden with its high, carefully clipped borders of shining box, its broad, smoothly gravelled walks; and its ~~wreath~~ of summer flowers. There was no sound save the chirping of the fearless little sparrows that hopped before him in the walk, busily gleaning their evening meal, and the faint lowing of the cows from the distant pastures. Mr. Clinton looked and listened in vain for any trace of Lilian, until turning into a side path he at length espied her.

At the extremity of the shaded alley was a white, latticed summer-house, covered with dark

green climbing plants. On the step, her childish
figure relieved against the deep shadow within,
sat Lilian, her head thrown back, her arm resting
around Great Heart's neck, who, couched behind
her on the floor of the arbor, his fore-legs hanging
over the step, lay, lazily blinking in sleepy content.

The dreamy look on the child's face flashed into
a glad smile as she sprang to meet Mr. Clinton,
while Great Heart, too indolent to follow, flapped
his tail heavily against the wooden floor, in patron-
izing welcome.

" What was my little girl thinking of? " asked
Mr. Clinton, as she slipped her hand into his.

" I wasn't thinking, I was feeling how beautiful it all is," she answered, drawing him towards
the alcoved summer-house. " Come and sit with
me here, and see the sunlight on the grass and
trees. I think this is the pleasantest part of all
the day. Nothing seems dark or cold that I think
of now ; even when I think of dying, I don't
feel afraid. Why is that ? "

" Perhaps because you know that the sun is
going to sink into darkness and silence, and yet
will rise again to-morrow morning, glorious as on
the first day," answered Mr. Clinton, looking tenderly down upon the sweet face, full of thought

and sentiment, that was turned so trustingly to
his.

"And now, Lilian, I have something to tell
you," he continued.

There was that in the tone of his voice which
arrested instantly her whole attention. It was a
tone deep, peculiar. She looked at him inquiringly. His serious eyes and dark face were lighted with a new expression.

"It is something good," she said. "Tell me."

"I am going to be married."

Lilian started from him as if he had struck her,
—stood for a moment, her eyes, dilated with pain,
fixed upon him,— then, without one word, darted
away.

Grieved, surprised, Mr. Clinton retraced his
steps. He knew the child so well, that he could
easily trace her sorrow to its source. "The poor
little thing thinks that I shall love her less," he
thought. "How little she knows me! There
would be no use in trying to console her now.
Later she will find out her mistake. But it pains
me."

And where was Lilian the while her best friend
was thoughtfully wending his way homeward beneath the spreading branches of the luxuriant

elms that bordered the road-side? In a vast, un-occupied garret, the one place where she was sure that no one would disturb her, Lilian, lost in a maze of misery, sat on the floor. "Mr. Clinton was going to be married; he would never care for her any more."

The red sunlight that struck upon the oaken beams overhead rose higher, grew fainter, and dis-appeared. Black shadows gathered in the remote corners, crept towards her, touched her, closed around her, still she did not move. Daylight and darkness were the same to her, drearily treading the aching circle of her inconsolable thoughts. At length the young moon appeared, and, through the window overhead, looked down upon her from the darkening sky. She raised her head, and saw it. Something changed the current of her thoughts. She gazed long and earnestly upward. Gradually the piteous look left her face. She rose slowly, and quitted her hiding-place.

Poor little Lilian!

VII.

"Miss Lilian, your grandmother wants you to come down-stairs. There's company wants to

see you," said Becky, entering Lilian's room, —
the large, sunny room, with its Brussels carpet of
ancient design, whereon gigantic roses and sober-
tinted scrolls mingled in inextricable confusion;
its paper of the date of the Empire, heavy pilas-
ters alternating with garlands of parti-colored
flowers, the whole bordered with a strange and
incongruous medley of golden quivers, sacrificial
rams' heads, and festoons of blue ribbons; its antiquated furniture, dark with age, brilliant with
constant rubbing, and resplendent with rows of
lions' heads, grinning, in burnished brass; its
ample snow-white draperies; its tall, narrow framed mirror, surmounted by a small funereal urn,
whence depended gilded wreaths of flowers (Lilian
had once nearly broken her neck in an attempt,
by means of an unsteady scaffolding of chairs and
footstools, to ascertain the mysterious contents of
that urn); its choice old engravings of the Ma-
donna of Dresden and the Last Supper, which she
contemplated every morning from her pillow with
adoring admiration and reverent compassion; —
into this large, sunny room, — the room where
Lilian had been born, — Becky entered as we
have said, much disturbing her little mistress,
who, curled up in the deep-seated embrasure of

the window, the light falling in flickering, green-ish-gold gleams upon her through the leaves of the great horse-chestnut-tree outside, was revelling in the wild wonders of the Arabian Nights.

" I wonder why the company always want to see me l " said Lilian, as she reluctantly closed the book and descended from her nook. " I am sure I don't want to see them! The gentlemen look at me until I feel ashamed, and the ladies talk about my clothes. I think it would do just as well to send in a dress for them to look at. I wish grandmamma would think so too."

" P'raps it would do for some folks," replied Becky, " but there's somebody there to-day who thinks more of you than he does of your clothes. Yes," she added, as Lilian gave a sudden start, " it's just Mr. Clinton and Mrs. Clinton, too. I caught a sight of her as she got out of the car-riage, and came up the steps. She's the beauti-fullest creature I ever saw in all my days."

With lingering steps and throbbing heart, Lilian descended the heavy staircase, paused a moment at the drawing-room door, then, with an unsteady hand, unclosed it, and entered. With downcast eyes, she advanced towards Mr. Clinton, and held out her hand. He took it, the chill little hand;

its trembling touch went to his heart. His eyes followed her solicitously, as, reluctantly, she approached and stood before his wife, — that dreaded usurper, who, vulture-like, had swooped down upon her peaceful life to rob her of its happiness.

" Look up, Lilian," said her grandmother.

She looked up, and saw, as in a vision, a seraph-like face, with deep blue eyes and locks of paly gold, bending towards her. A gentle arm drew her nearer, and a sweet voice whispered, —

" Will you not try to love me a little? I love you already, for Mr. Clinton has told me how much he loves you, and I love all that he loves, and all that love him."

As healing balsam on a poisoned wound, so fell the words, gently dropping with soothing iteration of the soft word, love, upon the child's sore heart. Timidly she fixed her eyes upon the lovely face before her, then shyly turned them towards Mr. Clinton, to meet a smile, a look, the brightest, the fondest, that had ever rested upon her. It was true! He loved her just the same! He looked as if he loved her even more! She forgot her jealous fears, her silent misery, her hidden tears. A flood of sunshine from within overflowed her. The pallid cheek flushed, the heavy eyes lighted, the relaxed corners of the mouth dimpled, the drooping figure rose erect. New life, like new wine, ran through every vein. Love was life to Lilian.

VIII.

" How does Lilian like my wife ? " asked Mr. Clinton on the next day, as she sat beside him — she was too tall now to sit on his knee — in the library.

" I like her very much," was the prompt reply ; " she's kind and she's beautiful. When I dream about angels, I see faces just like hers, only not so still. Why does she look so still even when she smiles ? "

Mr. Clinton paused before he answered, smoothing back the while Lilian's dark hair ; — it was a habit he still retained. " I will tell you," he said at last. " Mira's father was a selfish, dissipated man. Her mother, whom she loved exceedingly, was an invalid. Partly on account of her mother's health, but more on account of her father's habits, they lived abroad. Mira never had any fixed home, nor any playmates like other children. Her father gambled, and ran through the greater part of his fortune.

Mira and her mother underwent many privations. She was the only nurse her mother had. She was alone with her when she died. After her mother's death, her father placed her in a convent in Paris to finish her education. She was very unhappy there. She remained there several years. At length her father took her from the convent and brought her to America. Two months afterwards he was shot in a duel.— Now you know why she so rarely smiles, and why her face is so still. You must help me to make it brighter," he added, as Lilian's eyes swam in tears.

"I will try," said the child. "I will love her *so!*"

If there had still lurked any shade of jealousy in Lilian's mind, this conversation would have banished it effectually. She was now the fellow-laborer of Mr. Clinton in the endeavor to restore gladness to that fair, gentle creature, from whose heart early care and suffering seemed to have driven it forever.

—————

IX.

Lilian had said that she would love her; and yet, after many months of constant intercourse, the feeling which she cherished towards Mr. Clinton's wife could scarcely be called love, — it partook rather of the nature of adoration.

There was something intangible and unreal about the beautiful woman, that impressed the child with a vague sense of the supernatural. She was unlike any one· that Lilian had ever seen. Nothing external seemed to have power to affect her. She appeared devoid of human emotions. No passing cloud ruffled the unvarying calmness of her brow, no mirthfulness brought laughter to those placid lips. Lilian could not comprehend her. She had seen Mr. Clinton angry. Good as he was, she had marked his brow knit and his eyes flash when he was provoked. True, on those occasions he never spoke, yet she could well see that he was very angry. But Mira appeared inaccessible to any personal annoyance. It was not insensibility. She was full of tender thought and compassion for others. No tale of woe petitioned her pitying ear in vain. All gentle charities found her their willing ministrant. She lived as consecrated to the service of others, yet seemed ever far from them. There was the lovely form, the kindly thought, the helpful hand; but her innermost soul dwelt apart, distant as a star. When closest to her, Lilian felt that Mira's self was far away. As from infinite distance her calm look rested upon the child, as through regions of celestial space, her placid voice reached her ears.

Was Mira really a woman like other women, so Lilian often pondered, only far more beautiful and good? If so, how was it that she always seemed so like the vision of a woman.

It was only when she sang, that one could feel Mira's actual, undivided presence. When she sang! —

Have you ever turned aside from the glittering whirl of the fashionable promenade, the eddying rush of the crowded streets, or. the endless line of the gilded bazaars of some great foreign city, and, ascending the quiet steps and pushing aside the softly yielding portal of some Catholic church, entered its aisles, dim with misty shadow, lighted here and there with votive lamps? Have you, overlooking all difference of creed, feeling only that those around adored the One Great Father, mingled with the silent worshippers, thankful for the companionship of Faith and Prayer in a strange land; and while your heart melted, and your eyes moistened with the rush of solemn thought, has the great organ rolled its mighty waves of sound above your bended head, in majestic exultation, fuller and fuller, more and more glorious, till the arches echoed and the overhanging vaults trembled in unison? Then has the chorus risen, mingling with the pealing bass in many-voiced supplication, imploring, beseeching for mercy, for help, for pardon, in ~~even~~ more earnest entreaty? Cleaving its gathered fulness, have you heard one high, sweet voice soaring in celestial purity, higher and higher, sweeter and sweeter, clearer and clearer, till it seemed to reach the very gates of heaven, while you listened in breathless ecstasy, your whole soul suspended on the sound?—Such a voice was Mira's.

With clasped hands and parted lips, Lilian would sit in the twilight,—it was then Mira best loved to sing,—hanging on that voice of unearthly sweetness, chanting Geistliche Lieder, while the flickering firelight played in flashes upon Mira's gilded harp, her bending figure, and her upturned, transfigured face.

Sometimes a broader, higher gleam would show a tall, dark figure seated in the shade, his eyes fixed with an indefinable expression upon the rapt, unconscious singer.

Was Mr. Clinton wholly happy? Did that ethereal shadow satisfy the strong yearning of his heart? Could that lovely, snow-like image fill the young husband's arms?

Such questionings as these never entered Lilian's young mind; yet when she saw that look, she would dimly divine the presence of an unspoken pain, and stealing softly to his side, she would look up at him, her dark eyes full of unutterable affection; and Mr. Clinton's heavy brow would relax, and his compressed lips soften, as he met that loving, mutely-eloquent gaze.

Oh, wonderful love of children! Best balm after the love of God! Is any grief so dark that those holy eyes can shed no light upon it; so deep that those sweet, innocent voices can send no comfort to it; so hopeless that those loving, earnest hearts can bring no consolation to it? Little angels that stand at the entrance of our Valley of Humiliation, and, unknowing themselves of the message they bear, tell of God's light upon the mountain-tops, his glory upon the hills, and stretch their unspotted hands towards us, bidding us be of good cheer!

One evening they were alone. As the last strains of an ancient Catholic vesper-hymn vibrated on the air, Mr. Clinton rose, approached his wife, and bending over her, said in deep, troubled tones, —

" Mira, do you really love me ? "

" I love you," answered her gentle, passionless voice.

" With your whole heart ? " he urged in deeper, more troubled accents.

" I love God only with my whole heart," replied the sweet, clear, distant sounds. " I love you next to Him."

The husband answered not. He turned back and threw himself down on the sofa, his face turned towards the wall, while a hope died slowly, agonizingly, within him.

" You are very pale," said Mira, as at the end of an hour he rose and turned his face towards her. " Can I do nothing for you ? "

A faint, sad smile crossed his lips as he answered gently, —

" Nothing."

———◆———

X.

" I SHALL ride to town this morning," said Mr. Clinton as he laid aside his review, and rising from his easy-chair beside the breakfast-table with its service of old Sèvres, drew aside the damask curtain and looked out over the snowy landscape, glittering in the morning sun. He had grown fond of those long, lonely rides during these years of his married life.

Mira, who sat in her flowing dress of pale blue cashmere, busy with some delicate white embroidery, silently rose, left the room, and returned, bringing in her arms her husband's sable-lined coat and furred gauntlets. She placed them before the blazing fire, and advanced to his side.

"I fear you will be cold," she said, as she looked out with him over the snow-clad waste.

"I do not feel the cold without," he answered, fixing the indefinable look upon the Madonna-like face beside him.

He rang.

"Bid Rufus saddle Sylvia and bring her to the door."

The sound of hoofs was soon heard upon the gravel without. As Mr. Clinton descended the steps, his pretty favorite turned her head complainingly towards him. His quick eye ran over her graceful form and rested on her knees. They were cut and swollen.

“ What's this ? ” he exclaimed angrily, as he stooped to examine the injury. “ What's this ? ” he repeated still more angrily, as the lad who held the bridle hesitated to reply. “ Where's Rufus ? ”

“ Rufus told me to bring her, sir. He rode her from the blacksmith's last night, sir.”

“ Take her back to the stable, and tell Rufus to come here to me.”

As the lad retreated with the limping mare, Mr. Clinton opened his pocket-book, and selected some bank-notes. He looked up at the noise of heavily approaching steps. A dogged-looking groom stood before him, his eyes sullenly averted. Mr. Clinton handed him the folded notes and said, coldly, —

“ Here are your wages, Rufus. You may go.”

The gentleman turned and ascended the granite steps. The groom stood motionless until the hall-door had closed upon him, then raising his head, he cast after his master a vindictive look, and muttering between his clinched teeth a fearful oath, he also turned away.

“ Rufus has broken Sylvia's knees. I have dismissed him,” said Mr. Clinton throwing down his riding-whip as he reëntered the room where Mira still stood gazing over the landscape.

She turned with a look of sorrow in her eyes.

" Have you dismissed him? I am sorry for his wife and child. That little, sick child seems to be the only thing he cares for." And she glanced over the wide-spreading snow-drifts.

" There is no reason that they should suffer for his fault," her husband answered. " You will see that they are provided for. I shall take the train, and may not be at home till late. Good-by."

Mr. Clinton was not apt to retrace his steps. Was it a secret presentiment that brought him back yet once more? He returned. He stood before his wife. He took her hands in his. He gazed long and fondly on the transparent purity of her face, then bent, pressed a kiss upon her forehead, and was gone.

—◆—

XI.

THE short, brilliant winter day was drawing to its close. Towards the distant snow-clad hills, the large, red sun was slowly declining. Not in summer pomp of gold and purple, with crimson

drapery and silver sheen, was his evening pavilion
hung ; but in soft rose and tender lilac, as not to
shame the white shroud of the buried earth.   Still
and sharply defined against the pale flush of the
sky, rose the dark branches of the little wood
beside the icy river.   The last rays touched them
here and there with gold, — faint, lingering touches.
The sun dipped low, paused as for one last, guardian look, and disappeared.   A great shadow fell ·
cold and chill as he sank.

What moves among the brushwood by the
gleaming railroad track ? Is it man, or beast
that stirs only when the great Eye is withdrawn ?
What is that heavy, rolling sound ?

The bushes wave more wildly, they crack, they
break.   Forth from their covert looms an evil
form, — a man.   He glares cautiously around, then
turns to his task again.   Heaving with strength
amain, he pushes before him a large trunk, gray
and moss-grown.   Why has he raised it from its
quiet rest in the peaceful little wood ?   With la-
boring breath and straining muscle, he drives it
before him — good God ! — towards the railroad
track.   Prone it lies, unconscious messenger of
death, where the iron rails cross the river, deep,
swift-rushing under the ice.

The man stands erect. The sweat pours from his knotted brow like rain. He looks down the long, level, narrowing lines, and shakes his clinched fist above his head. He once more glares around, then plunges into the crackling brushwood, and is lost.

XII.

THE sunset light had faded from the west. The moon hung low in the cold, dark sky, shedding a light, ghastly in its distinctness, over the scene, as two muffled figures passed silently and quickly towards Rufus's cottage.

"I am sorry to keep you out after sunset," said Mira's voice, anxiously. "I had no idea it was so late. Do you feel cold?"

"Not very," answered Lilian; "and we can warm ourselves at the cottage; how cheerful it looks. Ah!"

A bright light suddenly filled the windows and flashed out upon the snow. A child's voice came in piercing shrieks through the icy air. They ran, they flew, they reached the cottage, they burst open the door.

The room was brighter than day, lighted by a

waving column of flame,—its base, the writhing body of a child. With agonized cries, it rushed towards Mira, its little arms outstretched. As the fiery death approached her, she tore open her heavy cloak, she caught the shrieking child in her arms, closed the thick folds around it, and threw herself on the floor, clasping it close; while Lilian's screams, and the child's smothered cries, rang through the suddenly darkened room.

Bending over her as she lay, by the faint firelight, Lilian could see Mira's brow contract, her eyes dilate, her lips tightly close, while the breath came heavily through the expanded nostrils. The flames had caught her sleeves. She but clasped the child the closer.

At length,—it seemed an age to Lilian,—Mira cautiously unclosed the mantle. All was dark beneath. She sprang to her feet, and lifted the moaning child on the bed.

"Snow, Lilian, quick, quick, snow!"

She covered its scorched and blistered arms and chest with soft, cold snow. As it melted from the raging burns, she renewed it, hanging over the tortured little creature with pitying words and tender caresses.

Gradually the soothing application lulled the

anguish of the child. Its convulsive movements
ceased; the contortion of pain left its face; it
moaned no longer, but lay quite still, its eyes
closed.

"Bring me more snow," whispered Mira, and
then run to my house, — it is the nearest, — and
send to the doctor to come here directly."

"Oh, Mira, your arms; will you do nothing
for your arms?" said Lilian, as she looked at the
tender arms, blotched with large, white blisters.

"Afterwards," answered Mira; and Lilian
sped away on her mission.

She was hardly gone, when a haggard, ferocious face was pressed from without upon the win-
dow-pane. Its fierce eyes rested upon the child.
It vanished in the fast-falling darkness, and Rufus
abruptly entered the room, and approached the bed.

"Do not be frightened, Rufus," said his mistress' gentle, compassionate voice. "She is not
very badly burnt."

"The lady put it out, father," said the child,
unclosing its eyes, and faintly smiling on the man.

Rufus looked at Mrs. Clinton. Her scorched
and dropping dress, her blistered arms, told him
all. He staggered for a moment, then, drawing
in his breath with a sharp, hissing sound, he smote

heavily upon his forehead, and fled from before that mild face, as Cain from the accusing sight of God.

With bounds like those of some hunted animal, he sprang towards the little wood beside the river. With superhuman speed he rushed. He devoured the ground. The ominous shriek of the fast-coming engine sounded each instant in his ears. The darkness looked blood-red to his eyes. Was he too late! His hell had begun. Remorse clutched him, tiger-like. He would have roared like the wild beast whose speed he had borrowed, but his dry throat and parched tongue refused utterance to sound. He gained the railroad. He bounded along the long, level, narrowing lines. Was that the red light far before him? Was that the fateful shriek? Was he indeed too late?

XIII.

Mira sat long beside the child, from time to time pondering Rufus's wild look, strange manner, and hurried flight! Her arms began to be intensely painful. How long the doctor was in coming! And Lilian, why did she not return? The child's mother, where could she be?

At length, Lilian appeared, deathly pale.

" I have sent for the doctor, and brought Becky
to take care of the child till its mother returns.
You must come home now, Mira," she said.   Her
teeth chattered as she spoke. Becky stood behind
her young mistress, silently, in the shadow. With
an authority in her manner Mira had never seen
before, Lilian wrapt her in the coverings that
Becky had brought, placed her arm around her,
and led her forth. Neither spoke, save when
Mira once breathed, " Thank God!" Lilian
shivered, and her teeth again chattered, as she
caught the words.

They reached the house. The hall-door stood
open. No servants were to be seen. Lilian opened
the door of the sitting-room. A fire blazed upon
the hearth. There was no other light. Seating
Mira on the sofa, she vanished and returned,
bringing bandages, liniments, and all the house
afforded. Without a word, she bound up Mira's
arms, then seated herself beside her. Mira took
notice of nothing. She was absorbed in her own
thoughts, — grateful, adoring thoughts, — as Lilian,
with a sharp pang, saw in the upward glance of
the fervent blue eye, and the tremulous quiver of
the parted lips.

At length, a rapid foot ascended the steps. The hall-door was flung open. Lilian started to her feet, and stood rigid, expectant, her eyes fixed upon the door. It opened, and Mr. Clinton, his dress torn, dripping, and dark stained, his face white as. that of a man who has seen Death face to face, stood in the door-way.

With a quick cry, Mira sprang towards him, while Lilian, with dry, gasping sobs, sank back into a chair.

———◆———

XIV.

THE early rays of the morning sun fell on the little wood and the icy river. Was that the peaceful little wood, and the smooth, ice-bound river, that wood of Desolation, that river of Death!

The snowy banks were trampled thick with marks of hurrying feet. The side of the bridge was wrenched and torn away. Below, choking the bed of the rushing river, which foamed and boiled around them, lay, piled in inextricable ruin, the burnished engine and gayly-painted cars,—one crushed, indistinguishable mass,—with broken fragments hurled wildly here and there. The cheerful sunlight played over them, as in mockery; but it fell on more than these. Crimson stains were on the crushed and upheaved ice, and broad and deep-sunk patches on the snow. Dread witness against the murderer;—innocent blood cried to God from the ground.

Upon the summit of the trampled bank, his eyes fixed immovably below, crouched the rough figure of a man. He heard not approaching steps. As a hand was laid upon his shoulder, he started violently, and rose to his feet. Rufus turned his haggard face and blood-shot eyes upon his master.

"I am glad to meet you, Rufus," said Mr. Clinton. "I have been already at your cottage, and am happy to find that your little girl is doing well. I wished to tell you that I take you back into my service. If there ever be any occasion on which I can serve you, you must let me know. You risked your life to save ours last night," he added, as he looked at the broken bridge and piled-up ruin. "I can never repay what I owe you;" and the gentleman held out his hand.

As his master spoke, the man's face grew livid; a ghastly spasm passed over it as he ended. He muttered a few words in a hoarse, inarticulate voice, then turned from the proffered hand, and hurriedly entered the wood.

" Poor fellow," said Mr. Clinton to himself, " I

should not have expected so much feeling from him." Then dismissing all thought of Rufus from his mind, he reverently uncovered his head, and, holding his hat before his face, stood for some minutes motionless.

Some hours later, Mr. Clinton sat by the bedside of his sleeping wife. The light came carefully shaded into the luxurious room, and hung back from the heavily-curtained bed, as fearing to disturb the sleeper. How beautiful she looked! Her golden hair had escaped from her muslin cap, and fell around her transparent face, pure in its pathetic beauty as that of an angel. Her husband sat and watched her.

A contraction disturbed the placid brow; her lips worked uneasily; she moaned. Suddenly, with an affrighted cry, she started from her pillow, her blue eyes staring wide in terror.

" I dreamed I stood on the bank of the little river below the bridge. A man, whose face I did not see, was beside me. There was no more water. The river ran blood. As I looked under the bridge, it began to heave, and I saw stiff, white hands pointing upwards out of the blood. Then dead bodies, in long, white shrouds, rose

6

slowly, each pointing one hand upward. They glided down the river, till they were opposite the man. Then they stood still. They fixed their eyes upon him. They raised their right hands, and pointed at him. They opened their mouths, as calling him, but I heard no sound. Then I perceived that the river of blood was swelling. It rose to the top of the bank, and the dead bodies began to move towards the man, as if to lay hold upon him. Then I screamed, and awoke."

" It was a frightful dream," said her husband. " Do not think of it. Let me tell you something that will please you. I have taken Rufus back. That is not all that I shall do for him. You do not know that he risked his life to save ours last night. He came rushing along the track to warn us, but it was too late."

Mira's lips turned white; her eyes closed; she sank back on her pillow.

Mr. Clinton, alarmed, hung over her with anxiously proffered help.

" Only to be alone," she breathed, faintly; " only to be alone!"

As the door closed, she opened her eyes, full of unutterable horror. Conviction glared before her. She knew the murderer. His life was forfeit to

the laws. Should she denounce him? Should his
blood be upon her head?

She wrung her hands. Doubt and Dismay laid
hold upon her. Horror and Compassion wrestled
within her. She prayed for guidance. She prayed
in vain. A thick veil fell upon her mind. The
power of thought seemed leaving her. Monstrous
images of possible crime possessed her imagination; and through all she saw close before her the
wolfish face that had glared in upon her from the
darkness of the night before. She pressed her
hands before her eyes, to shut out the sight. She
cried with a bitter cry to God for aid. Then calm
came upon her, and she heard, as it were, a voice,
saying, "Love your enemies; do good to them
that hate you, and pray for them that despitefully
use you and persecute you."

The reaction of extreme excitement had come.
One of the sacred sentences with which her memory was filled rose uppermost, borne soothingly in
on her mind by one of the mysterious processes
through which Nature seeks to restore our mental
equilibrium when she sees danger in its longer
disturbance.

But Mira received the words as sent from
Heaven,— the pulseless calm, as the sign and
pledge of God's guidance and blessing.

She knelt devoutly, and promised, as in His presence, to protect the murderer.

———◆———

XV.

THE snow melted. The accusing stains sank into the unrevealing bosom of the earth. Soft, tufted grass, with white anemones and purple violets, replaced the trampled tracks of hurrying feet. The river rushed free under the bridge. The little wood waved as peacefully as if it had never echoed to the groans of the dying, or the wailing of the living above the dead. All deathful tokens had disappeared from that tranquil spot, seldom visited, save by that man who steals towards the bank, in the late evening, or by earliest dawn, and listens, and peers over the brink. Does he hear aught, save the rushing of the water? Does he see aught, save grass and wild flowers? What brings him there alone?

———◆———

XVI.

"LILIAN, come in here," said Mr. Clinton, opening the library door, as he heard her light step in the hall.

"I want to speak to you," he continued, as he

handed her to a chair, but without sitting down himself. He stood leaning against the mantel-piece. He looked careworn.

"How does Mira seem to you?" he said at length, with evident effort.

"Not very well," answered Lilian, slowly.

There was a long pause. At length, he spoke again,—

"I am going to ask you to do me a great favor. I want you to come here to stay with us, to be continually with her. You are intelligent beyond your years. She loves you. She will be happier if you are here. He paused a moment, and continued: "You have seen how timid she has become."

"Yes," said Lilian, in a low voice.

"Since the night of the accident, and of her efforts to save that child, she has seemed borne down by continual terror. She gives no reason for it. Any reference to it distresses her. I cannot understand it. The physicians can throw no light upon it. The shock seems to have destroyed her nerves." He stopped, and groaned aloud. "Lilian, I fear for her reason." He walked abruptly to the window.

The young girl rose. She moved a few steps

toward him, then stopped, and stood waiting. He returned presently, calm, as was his wont.

"I knew it all," she said; "I will come." She took his hand in both of hers, and looked up in his face. "If I could only comfort you!"

Mr. Clinton stooped, kissed her forehead as when she was a child, and turned hastily away.

From that hour, Lilian never quitted Mira's side. She received her as a trust from Mr. Clinton. She devoted her life to fulfilling that trust. She read to her, she chatted with her, she sat silently beside her, always in Mira's sight. She drew back the curtains everywhere, and let broad floods of sunlight into the rooms. She decked them with flowers. She filled the windows of Mira's sitting-room with tropical birds of gorgeous plumage and sweetest song. She taught Great Heart to couch by Mira's side, while she played to her grand, soul-stirring, strength-giving harmonies.

Her fresh, young life filled the overclouded house with a new atmosphere. Mira felt its influence. The ever-watchful care, the feminine tact, the gentle gayety that surrounded her, insensibly lessened the weight of her horrible secret. Sometimes, for a while, she would forget it. The look of tension in her eyes relaxed. Her nervous start became less frequent. Her apprehensive lips once more closed placidly. Lilian would sometimes flatter herself that the mysterious cloud had rolled away; but again Mira's face would curdle with horror, her cheeks and lips turn white, her hands grow icy cold. Then Lilian would silently throw her arms around her, press her warm cheek to Mira's quivering lips, and hold the cold hands in hers. As the agony relaxed, Mira would press Lilian tightly to her, as thankful for human companionship, and, shivering, bury her face in Lilian's neck. Once Lilian had said, " Tell me, Mira." But Mira had suddenly pushed her away, exclaiming, with unnatural vehemence, " Don't tempt me!" Then breaking into hysterical sobs, she had murmured, " Oh, God, help me to hold fast!" What could this terror mean? What was the frightful mystery that was thus torturing this innocent creature, — killing her before their eyes?

" Go into the garden, Lilian," said Mr. Clinton, in a low voice. " I will watch by her till you return. You begin to look pale."

And taking the place which Lilian yielded to him, he sat beside the sofa, and again watched his sleeping wife, — lovely still, but how woe-worn, how changed!

Lilian, followed by the patient Great Heart, walked slowly down the broad, sunny walk. The air was filled with the odors, busy with the murmuring hum of spring. She noticed not these things. Her heart was heavy within her. She saw no end to the misery. Vainly she strove once more to unriddle the mystery.

"What can it be?" burst from her lips.

A stealthy step approached her. Great Heart stopped short, and growled. She looked up, and saw Rufus. His cheeks were hollow, his eyes glittered.

"Did you call me?" he said, peering into her face.

"No," answered Lilian, drawing back.

He glanced restlessly around; then, looking down at his feet, changed his place uneasily. Lilian, somewhat startled, moved on.

"Take care," he exclaimed; "you'll tread in that spot!"

"What spot? Where?" asked Lilian, her heart beginning to beat fast.

"There, just before you." And coming close he whispered, "*It's blood!*"

Lilian's pulses stopped. Her knees shook under her. — He was mad!

She glanced around to see if any help were at hand. She saw the coachman hurrying up the walk. Rufus's eyes wandered glittering around. Suddenly their look fixed, was concentrated as on some invisible object. He stretched his head forward, as if listening intently.

" Yes, yes, I'm coming," he whispered. And with long, striding leaps, the haunted wretch sprang away.

" Did Rufus speak to you, Miss ? " said the coachman, touching his hat as he came up to where Lilian, violently trembling, stood leaning against a tree.

" He asked me if I had called him, and said that there was blood on the ground. What is it ? Is he mad ? "

" I'm afraid he is, Miss. He's been queer for some weeks ; a muttering to himself, and a listening as if he heard something ; and this morning I found him scouring where there was nothing to scour, and whispering that he couldn't get up the spots. But I must be after him, Miss, or he'll do himself or somebody else a mischief." And again touching his hat, the coachman took the direction in which Rufus had fled.

Mira still slept, — her husband still watched by her, — while Lilian sat in the recessed window, impatiently waiting to speak to Mr. Clinton, yet not daring to run the risk of disturbing the sleeper.

A heavy hurried step sounded along the hall, and a knock came at the door. Mr. Clinton rose and went out, leaving the door ajar. Lilian started up and listened with straining ears. She could only catch a few words, " bank, — river," — then the voice sank, and she listened in vain till it rose with the last, — " his throat cut."

Sick and faint she sat down again as Mr. Clinton reëntered the room. Lightly as he closed the door, the sound awoke his wife. She looked from his face to Lilian's.

" Something has happened! What is it! Tell me, oh tell me," she prayed, joining her hands; — the haunting look of terror in her eyes.

Mr. Clinton approached her.

" Yes, something has happened that will distress you," he said. " Rufus is dead."

Mira sprang to her feet, extended wide her arms.

" *It was he !* "

As the hoarse unnatural accents sounded on

their startled ears, the weight she sought to raise from her heart, crushed back upon her brain. She groaned and fell heavily forward into her husband's arms.

----•----

XVII.

THE house on the hill is closed. All is cold, cheerless order within. Wander through the deserted rooms, — you will find no sunlight, no birds, no flowers now. Open door after door, — all is equally chill, formal, and silent, no sign of life. — But yes! Here in the library burns a cheerful fire. In the great, green, easy-chair sits a slender girl, bending over a heavy volume, intent, absorbed. An old stag-hound lies stretched out before the fire. His feet move, keeping time to his sleeping thoughts. He dreams that he is young again.

The light begins to fade. The girl lays down the heavy volume. She rises, goes to the window and looks out.

Autumn is passing into winter. Its gorgeous tapestry has fallen from the trees. The scarlet maple no longer blazes beside the golden walnut. The dark-red foliage of the oak lies withering on the ground. The sky is drear. Quick, eddying gusts of wind drive the dry leaves before them down the hill.

" November, December, January, February, March, April, May, — seven months before I see them again."

She replaces the book on the shelf, sighs as she looks around her, prepares for her homeward walk, rouses the reluctantly awakening, slowly stretching dog, and wends her way down the hill, past the gray little church and quiet graveyard, towards her home.

—◆—

XVIII.

" Oh for heaven's sake, ma'am, come quick," cried Becky, bursting into her mistress's room. " Come quick to Miss Lilian, something's the matter ! "

And followed by the terrified grandmother, she hurried back to where Lilian sat, her hands rigidly grasping a newspaper, her throat convulsively working. She neither stirred nor spoke in answer to her grandmother's affrighted exclamations.

" Oh, read it, ma'am, — it's something in the

paper that's done it," said Becky, bursting into tears.

No sooner was the paper touched, than, as if a spell had been broken, Lilian started up and fell on her knees in an agony of wild sobs. Her grandmother read, —

" Melancholy shipwreck and loss of life. We regret to learn that the yacht Nereid was run down on the night of the 17th ult. off the Bay of Naples, by the Neapolitan steamer Ercolanes, bound from Naples to Marseilles. All on board the yacht perished with the exception of the owner, Mr. Clinton, U. S. A., who was picked up severely injured.

XIX.

YEARS passed, — those momentous years which change the child into the woman. Where now were those that Lilian loved ? Mira was dead, drowned in the bright blue sea. The sunny shades of Asia had closed over Mr. Clinton. He was a wanderer. None knew when he would return. The vapid, empty-minded society in which her grandmother delighted was void of interest to Lilian. Her heart, unable to ex-

pand, sent its vigor to her intellect. Books became her chosen counsellors, her familiar friends.
Fleeing the monotonous round of ceremonious
civilities which absorbed her grandmother, she
took refuge in the deserted library. There, within those silent walls, eloquent with memories,
the happiest hours of her young solitary life were
spent.

The free range of an English library ! It was
a trying ordeal for a young girl's mind. The
works of the authors whom Mr. Clinton had
chosen for her once exhausted, she was left to
wander unguided amid the labyrinth.

Through the luxuriant garden of the old English literature she strayed unharmed, shielded by
her virgin innocence of mind. Crouching among
the flowers, lurking beside the sweet waters, hiding
in the pleasant shades, she saw many a toad, many
a vile, creeping thing ; but safe in the absence of
the Ithuriel spear of consciousness, she passed un-
heeding on, deeming them perchance unlovely,
but unwitting of the devil hidden within. With
white feet she trod unscathed among the burning
pages of the authors of the Regency. With pure
eyes she looked on all, and it was pure.

Her mind grew and gathered strength. Her

taste developed and ripened. Her sympathies widened and deepened. Her heart long forgot its loneliness in the richness of her intellectual life.

But as she grew into the grace of womanhood a vague melancholy overshadowed her. The longing for a greater happiness pursued her. An indescribable atmosphere of sadness hovered about her, whence her deep, soft eyes looked imploringly forth.

What did she seek? What did she wish? She knew not. And thus she sat under the old oak-tree, reading the Prologue to " Faust," when we first saw her.

She had not perceived the approach of a stranger, so soft was the grass under his feet, so absorbing was the poem. It was only when he advanced and stood before her, that she raised her eyes. With a glad cry she started up and sprang to meet him with outstretched hands and radiant face.

" Mr. Clinton! Oh, I am so glad!" She stopped, her countenance changed, her voice sank. " I am so " ——

A rigid, speech-forbidding look passed over the dark face before her. She comprehended, and was silent.

"You are much changed. You are no longer my little Lilian," he said, still holding her hand, as his eye travelled observantly over the low, broad forehead, shaded by bands of thick, soft hair; the large, dark, shadowy eyes, the delicate outline of the nose, the spirited nostril with its warm shadow, the rich, purely curved lips with their look of sweet reserve, the proud chin, the smooth line of the untinted cheek, the indescribable grace and symmetry of early womanhood in her figure.

"I am sorry," she answered regretfully.

"Sorry! Do you not know that you are much more beautiful now?"

"I am sorry to have lost the face that you were fond of."

Mr. Clinton smiled on the lovely face that looked up pleadingly at him. Her heart grew light. He might deny it, but she felt that she was still his little Lilian.

He stooped and raised the book that she had let fall in rising. He looked at the title. He did not give it back.

"My child, this is no book for you to read." And he fixed his eyes inquiringly upon her. Her look met his frankly.

" Is it not ?   I found it in the library, and you know that I have no one " —   She paused.

" Yes, I know," he responded sadly, and he gazed thoughtfully upon her earnest face. — Might he not find here the occupation his aching mind needed ? "

He had travelled in vain.   He had looked upon the Pyramids.   On the highest summit a veiled form stood and vanished into the evening sky. He sought the great Victoria water, far in the untrodden Southern wilds.   From amid the roar of the falling torrent, rose a cry as of a woman drowning.   He rested under the ruins of Eastern temples.   Deep blue eyes gazed upon him from the shade.   He crossed the trackless desert. Slender footprints marked the scorching sands. He had returned, hopeless of forgetfulness, to bear his burden as best he might.   And here stood before him the child he had so much loved, grown into a woman more lovely still, fatherless, motherless, solitary, — for he knew her and the influences around her.   He felt that, as when a little child, she was still very lonely.

Thus they stood, hand in hand, busied with many thoughts.   He broke the silence.

" You say that you have no one.   You shall

be my little Lilian, if you like, and I will teach you.

She started with delight. The blood rushed to her cheek, her eyes filled with light.

"How good you are! How happy I shall be!"

XX.

A NEW life opened before Lilian, — a life of gentle contentment and lofty thought. Her little blue draperied sitting-room, with its long Venetian window, opening on the flower-garden, its cottage pianoforte, and small round table, became to her a very temple of happiness. Mr. Clinton's protecting care and quiet affection were ever present with her. His intelligent sympathy doubled the keenness of her perceptions. His vigorous mind moved, a pillar of strength beside her, in every arduous pass. He led her to the highest, purest sources of Art and Philosophy. With fresh, eager lips, she drank deep of Grecian springs. The divine wisdom of Plato, like music of the spheres made audible, — the subtle analysis of Aristotle, keen and searching as a two-edged sword, — the wild fancies of Pythagoras, — the sweet wisdom of Epicurus, — the lofty heroism of

Zeno, — rolled upon her soul in golden harmonies of antique speech.

The many-voiced chorus in accordant unison, rising and falling in alternate resounding waves, — the classic majesty, the tender grace, the compass- ed passion, the soul-compelling pathos, the stern self-devotion of those colossal creations which breathe from ancient pages the same deathless life now as when the crowded theatres of buried cities first rose to acclaim their birth, — with stately, superhuman motion passed before her. Bending forward with hushed lips and awed look, she hung upon his voice, as in deep cadence it fell upon her rapt, delighted ear. Unheard the music of the birds without, the summer rustling of the leafy trees, the song of the mowers faint rising from the distant fields, she listened, and her heart rose high ; — it swelled to burst the limits of the life around her, to break forth into noble speech and nobler deeds. The enthusiasm of the Good and the Beautiful was upon her. A godlike life filled her soul!

And he, the teacher, how did he look upon the beautiful girl whose hidden treasures of heart and mind were laid so trustingly open to his attentive eye?

She was still to him his little Lilian, — nothing
more.

Not only in the sunny morning was Mr. Clinton there. In the quiet, starlight evening, when
the shaded lamp filled the softly-tinted room
with dreamy light, through the wide-opened window resting on the dark, glistening leaves, and
rich odor-breathing flowers motionless without, he
would walk forth, — down the slope of the hill,
through the hushed woods, beside the dark ravine,
across the sleeping meadows, — to Lilian's garden
and her quiet room. It was the hour she gave to
music.

Shading his face from even the shaded lamp, he
would sit, while the deep, unearthly harmonies of
Beethoven, the sad, far-reaching fantasies of Cho-
pin, the massive fugues of Bach, the enticing melo-
dies of Mozart, the penetrating sweetness of Men-
delssohn, the imploring improvisations of Henselt,
poured forth upon the night, bearing him out from
the haunting pressure of his grief, into that great
universe of higher thought, where Time becomes
Eternity, and Space is lost in Infinity. Then
soothed, refreshed, he would again pass forth into
the starlight, and regain the solitary home, where

no gentle voice, no loving eyes, awaited him, to study till the stars grew dim.

* * *

XXI.

IT was earlier than his wont. Mr. Clinton sat on the rustic seat beneath the great tree which grew below Lilian's garden. A deeper sadness than usual oppressed him. He had come to seek companionship, but, with the caprice of a sick heart, he had turned aside when his feet had borne him where he had wished to be.

A deep, sad symphony floated through the air. A sweet, rich voice took up the strain —

"Einsam wandelt dein Freund im Frühling's Garten."

Thrilling through the twilight stillness, full of eternal longing, of deathless pain, —

" Adelaida ! "

Could it be Lilian ! He rose and advanced unseen towards the window.

The song of resurrection breathed from her lips. Again, but in immortal hope, in sublimest exultation, —

" Adelaida ! "

Mr. Clinton leaned against the window. The memory of lost hopes pierced him through and through. She had given it voice, and the expression of his pain had rendered it all but unendurable.

Lilian turned and saw his face. She felt all that her song had done. She bent over the piano, and her tears fell slow and heavy on the ivory keys.

The night breeze came sweeping over the flowers. It raised, as with loving fingers, the heavy curls from his brow; it softly caressed his cheek; it pressed in invisible waves upon his lips. It seemed to rock and lull his pain.

He entered the room. Lilian dared not look up at the manly figure, the noble face before her. He took her hand.

" Good-night, my child."

And Lilian found herself alone.

Like a culprit, on the next morning, she waited for his coming.

He came,—a shade graver than usual, perhaps; otherwise the same.

And the evening starlight brought him, as was his wont. He seated himself, with folded arms and head erect, as ready to meet a foe.

" Sing to me, Lilian," he said.

She obeyed. Her tones were low and faltering at first; but gradually the music bore her up, as on strong wings, above the consciousness of his presence. Deep, full, steady, rose her voice, swelling into grandeur, softening into pathos. She breathed her soul forth in melody rich and rare.

The music ceased. As one who, though sorely wounded, comes victorious from a conflict, Mr. Clinton met Lilian's half-frightened glance. She comprehended what had passed within him. She never feared to sing to him again.

XXII.

.THE spring and early summer were past. The scythe.of the mower had swept over the pleasant fields, — their wealth of green, their joy of flowers, — and they had lain sere and desolate. But again the tender grass appeared, and blossoms, richer, sweeter than those which had perished, sprang from their bosom.

And a second spring, a second summer, came to the heart of Mr. Clinton.

Imperceptibly, as gentle morning changes to puissant noon, softly as dewy spring waxes to fer_ vent summer, did the affection he felt for the young girl grow into love. It grew and gathered strength, as in enchanted silence. The shadow of his grief melted away. A deeper light filled his eyes, a sweeter smile played around his lips, a new gladness warmed his heart. But he knew not that he loved.

—◆—

XXIII.

IT was mid-day. Mr. Clinton sat in the little blue-draperied room. Lilian, on a low seat before the open window, her face turned towards him, read aloud.

The glory of summer sunlight without rested upon the outlines of her white draped figure, and illumined the shadow through which he saw her face.

She read the Tempest. The sweet, persuasive music of her voice filled the room with soft waves of melody. Gradually Mr. Clinton's look, dwelling with gentle interest upon her, deepened, concentrated. A trouble passed over his face. The sweet voice flowed on. A quick tremble ran through his powerful frame. The voice paused, — then soft, searching, thrilling through his awakening soul, Lilian's lips breathed forth Miranda's words, —

" Do you love me ? "

Mr. Clinton rose and took the book from Lilian's hands.

" It is enough," he said, in a low voice.

As one in a dream, he reached his own house, and threw himself down to think.

" Do you love me ? " The sweet voice was ever in his ears, the gentle face before his sight.

Yes, he loved her. Like that rare tropical flower which slowly through long years grows within its enfolding leaflets, then in one instant bursts into its rich, luxuriant perfection, so his unconscious, silently evolving love, at those words opened upon him. It filled his whole being, — it spread, it filled the universe.

His life became love of her. He loved her with a love vivid, yearning, intense, soft with a tenderness, glowing with a passion such as he had never known before. All the forces of his nature, deepened by years of solitude and revery, drew towards her. The fountains of his heart were broken up. Its affections poured forth upon her in a mighty flood.

Her presence dazzled him. He closed his eyes

not to see her. Her breath intoxicated him. He placed space between them, that he might not suffocate. He sat no more beside her. The mere thought of touching her hand made him shiver from head to foot. And yet the possibility of winning her never entered his mind. She, the beautiful girl who looked up to him as to a father! No. It was but the exchange of one suffering for another. He was used to pain. He could bear it. When he could bear it no longer, he would go. Meantime all should be as it was before.

Nothing betrayed to Lilian the tumult within Mr. Clinton. She might have noticed, perhaps, that he spoke less than before; that her studies insensibly assumed a severer cast; that he was graver, and seemed sometimes absorbed in thought. But his tone was as gentle, his smile as kind as ever. It was some cloud of memory that overshadowed him. She wished that she could make him forget. She wished that she could make him happy.

No sign told her that her voice sent the blood coursing through his veins, that her smile made his senses reel. She gathered flowers on the brink of a volcano, and joyed in the soft white cloud that hid the furnace below.

So time passed on, in frank, childlike affection on her part, in absorbing passion on his, severely controlled without, — the fiercer within.

——◆——

XXIV.

IT was evening. Lilian had been singing to Mr. Clinton. His eye had dwelt upon her lovely profile, her deep-set, earnest eyes, her lips so soft, so full of sentiment, the delicate symmetry, the luxuriant grace of her form, until he felt that her beauty would drive him mad. . The time had come. He must leave her!

He approached and took her hands in his. He spoke. It was in a hoarse, suppressed tone that she had never heard before.

" Lilian — I am going away. — I dare not stay. Farewell ! "

Was it rapture or agony that ran along her every vein, that thrilled through her every nerve at his touch? His look compelled hers. She slowly raised her head. His eyes blazed into her own. Her heart beat in heavy shocks. One instant ! — He was gone ! — He had taken her soul.

XXV.

THE gray dawn found Lilian sitting in her bedroom, — stunned, bewildered, wretched. She knew that she loved Mr. Clinton; and he was gone. He did not wish to love her, did not wish her to love him. He had left her. — She could not believe in her own misery. It could not be true. It must be some frightful dream. The morning would come, and she would see him again. It could not be that he would leave her!

She rose and threw open the window as if to dissipate her wretchedness. Her eye rested on an angle of the road. As she looked absently down, she heard the sound of rapidly rolling wheels. A travelling-carriage was whirled along. She recognized it. It was his. She turned back and threw herself face downward across her bed. The daylight was hateful to her. She lay long in a dim stupor of misery. At length the stir of the house told her that the long day had begun. She arose, changed her dress, arranged her hair, and descended to the breakfast-room, drearily thankful that her grandmother's imperfect sight would not suffice to read the expression of her face.

As she was busy with the urn, a servant brought in a note and presented it to her grandmother. Lilian felt from whom it came. She longed to snatch it from the silver salver. Her grandmother put on her spectacles, slowly unfolded and read it, then, looking at Lilian, said in her impassive manner, —

" A note from Mr. Clinton. He says that he is suddenly obliged to leave home, and that he is uncertain how long he shall be gone."

She stopped. Lilian made no answer. Her grandmother continued, —

" I suppose you'll miss him for a while. But on the whole, though he certainly was very kind to you, and I daresay taught you a great deal, I'm glad he has gone, for, now I look at you, you are getting as pale as a ghost ; — not that you ever had much of any color, but you didn't use to look as you do now. And you must look your best this winter, for your coming out, you know."

And her grandmother tore up the note, that Lilian would have given worlds to have rescued, and turned it into little white allumettes.

XXVI.

A FEVERISH restlessness laid hold upon Lilian. One controlling desire beset her, one longing hope pursued her, — to hear something of him, — to know something of him, — to see him once more.

She waited impatiently for the time when they should be established in the city for the season. She would be more apt to hear of him there. She knew that he had intended to spend a part of the winter in town. Perhaps he would still do so. She should meet him then. To see him once more! — That hope bounded her horizon.

An element of coquetry developed itself in her mind. His approbation had become so dear to her! — With new-born interest she studied her face in the mirror. She saw that she was beautiful. She listened attentively to her grandmother's projects for her toilet. Her beauty must be arrayed so as best to please his eye. — Her heart wellnigh failed her as she opened her piano-forte, but her hand must be pliant, her voice be clear, that she might delight his ear when they met.

Her beauty increased. The statue-like purity of her cheek wore a more touching sweetness, her soft, dark eyes, filled with unuttered thoughts, were deeper; — her lips had something imploring in their sensitive curves. A tremulous atmosphere of unsatisfied unrest surrounded her, like the quivering around a star.

XXVII.

THE ground was frozen beneath her feet, the last dry leaves had been swept away by the winter wind, large flakes of snow fell slowly and as at random from the sad, gray sky, and rested on Lilian's closely-robed figure as she passed towards the gray, little church below the hill. Into the graveyard, — between the mossy tombstones, — she stands by her parents' graves. She stands long, unmindful of the hurrying flakes, the frozen ground, the biting cold. She .stoops. She gathers two little leaves from the graves. She presses them to her lips. She hides them in her bosom. She passes on to a newer grave, a grave empty of all save loving memories. Surrounded by closely-planted cypresses as if, even in this secluded spot, to shade it from every eye, lies a marble slab, —

"SACRED TO THE MEMORY OF MIRA,
WIFE OF HARVEY CLINTON.
AGED 21 YEARS."

Long she gazed on the pure, white stone. The snow-flakes fell fast and faster. They lay thick upon the slab. They spread in a broad, white sheet over it. With soft touches they effaced the inscription. Then Lilian with a sense of strange relief, turned away.

She gathered no leaf from that grave, — yet she had loved ·Mira well.

——◆——

XXVIII.

THE whirl of the great city received Lilian. Society opened its arms eagerly to her. She was new ! She was beautiful ! She sang like an angel ! She belonged to one of its " best families ! " — It fêted her, it caressed her, it flattered her.

Her success was doubled by the queenly indifference of her bearing. For a new change had come over Lilian. She looked upon the world as an ambushed foe. She dreaded lest some chance eye should descry her secret, some careless word gall her misery. She lived as one who feels that at any moment he may be called upon to defend his life. She wrapt herself in an icy reserve, through which her beauty shone like the moon through a frosty sky. Her chilling reticence but fanned the eagerness of her admirers like a cold wind passing over fire. There was something about her peculiarly fascinating to men. Her charms of person, her cultivation of mind and manner, her sensitive temperament, and above all, her inaccessibility, irresistibly attracted them ; — they pursued her.

The admiration that she excited, tormented Lilian ; her soul filled with one all-absorbing affection. To her there was but one man in the world. All others were as painted, moving images. Their conversation fatigued her, their attentions displeased her, their compliments vexed her. She felt their declarations as an insult to her love. They called her la bella ~~Chiacceinola~~, and adored her.

It was only towards young girls that she thawed. To them she was invariably gentle and affectionate. She looked down upon their rosy group as from an immeasurable height of woe. There was a touching intonation in her voice when she addressed them, a veiled compassion in her manner. The sunlight gladdened them, life smiled before them, hope delighted them, as once they had done her. She wondered if they would ever suffer as she did. She pitied them for the possible grief that lay before them.   Her face wore a pathetic sweetness when she looked upon them, as if they had been innocent, ill-fated children.

With girlish enthusiasm they admired her. They raved about her.   Cold!— They would not hear the word.   She was the loveliest, sweetest creature in the .world.   Haughty!— They grew indignant.   She was the gentlest of created beings.   What did the men mean?   Did they want her to marry them all?

They surrounded her wherever she appeared with their smiling eyes, their laughing lips, their delighted greetings; till the black habits assembled around their flower-crowned group, closed in, broke it, and encircled Lilian, pale, beautiful, and icy.

And the rush of the great world bore her ever on, tasking her ear to catch amid its busy murmur an echo of one name; straining her eye to seize a glimpse among the hurrying crowd, of one stately figure, one noble face.   Listening, searching ever.   Listening, searching ever in vain.

Each day she detested more the life she led, the position she held.   She was oppressed, stifled. She wearied of speech, of the frivolous, unmeaning conversation in which she was compelled to bear her part. At every moment to speak, and yet to be dumb forever!

But there were moments when she felt snatched into solitude, when she dared to break the silence of her heart. Safe in the loneliness of music, her pent-up misery overflowed before those around her, and they knew it not. Pleading, imploring, anguished, rose her voice, under the dazzling lamps, amid the rare exotics, above the brilliant crowd hanging delighted on those pathetic tones. And with its wonted penetration the world admired her power as an actress. "What an exquisite voice! What wonderful expression! Who would have expected so much feeling from her quiet, cold manner! What a prima donna she would make!"

XXIX.

ONE evening she sat in a little rose-colored boudoir. From the adjoining rooms came the murmur of gay voices, the sound of music and of dancing feet.

Lilian was too wretched that evening to act her part. She could not dance. She could not

talk. " Should she never see him again!" She
had pleaded headache, and her pitying hostess
had placed her in the little rosy boudoir, and forbidden her guests to intrude.

On a table near her, lay books of engravings
and a rich album. She opened it half unconsciously. Her thoughts had wandered to another
room, blue tinted, far away. Mechanically she
turned over the leaves of the book before her.
It was full of pencil sketches, hurried but spirited, — sketches of Greece. Suddenly the blood
rushed in a torrent to her brow and cheek. What
was on the opening page? What did she see?
His face, — his own, — his very own! She
gazed upon it as the shipwrecked mariner on
land.

" Isn't it a splendid head?" said a gay voice
beside her. " The sketch is good for nothing.
— (I wonder why my mother will keep that book
here!) It's not half so handsome as he is. He's
a superb fellow, — Harvey Clinton. I suppose
you don't know him, he's been away so much.
He's one of my best friends. He saved my life
there, in Greece. I met him in Athens. I
asked leave to join him. I didn't much think he
wanted me, but he let me come. It was just

after that dreadful accident; perhaps you may have heard of it. His yacht was run down and his wife drowned. He hadn't got over it at all. They say he never has. — But I was saying he saved my life. I fell ill up in the mountains; — worst place in the world to be ill in, — miserable huts, — people all robbers. I was never so ill in my life. At the end of the first day I couldn't stand. So provoking too! — Knocked all his plans on the head. — Well, — he took care of me as if he had been my mother. I shouldn't have believed that any man could have been so tender. Such a tall, athletic fellow as he is too. I was ill enough, but he brought me through. I'll never forget it!" And handsome Charley Prevost's happy blue eyes filled for an instant with tears.

"What a fool she'll think me!" he thought to himself, but as he glanced at Lilian his apprehensions vanished. Her head was gently turned towards him, her eyes smiling, her lips sweet, her cheek flushed.

"By Jove, what a beauty she is!" he mentally exclaimed; and handsome Charley, already smitten, made a deep plunge forward in the process of falling in love.

And Lilian, innocently, unconsciously lured him on.

He loved Mr. Clinton! He became to her different from the rest of the men around her. Her coldness vanished. She welcomed him with a smile when he approached her. She listened with attentive ear when he talked to her, waiting the while expectantly for some reference to him she loved. She allowed him to wait upon her, to follow her. She thought only of Mr. Clinton. Handsome Charley thought only of her.

The world observed, commented, and approved. " A very good match on both sides. I wonder when it will come out ! "

XXX.

It was a full opera-night. The house was crowded. Every one was there. The first act had ended when Lilian and her grandmother entered their box. The murmur which always attends the entrance of the reigning belle ran round the house. Every eye was turned upon her, as she stood, robed in pale green, her ermine cloak falling from her shoulders, a wreath of oak-leaves in her braided hair. She bent her head slightly in answer to the salutations of those nearest, took her seat, and turned her eyes slowly, searchingly around. He was not there.

Look again, Lilian. Far back in the shadow of the box below who is that who bends his eyes immovably upon you! He is changed. He looks worn and stern, but do you not know him?

He watches her as the young men throng to pay their court. He marks with secret joy her calm indifference, her cold reserve. She cares for none of those!

The door of the box again opens. He knows well that gay, young face. It is his old travelling-companion, handsome, good-natured Charley Prevost. Ah! Lilian knows him well also! Her eyes brighten, she smiles, she holds out her hand, she allows him to take the seat behind her. She listens attentively to what he is saying.

Mr. Clinton's brow knits, his lips are firmly compressed. It is what he had told himself over and over again, would, must happen. Lilian would be loved, and would love. It was natural, it was right, — but it was unendurable! As fascinated by his own pain, he stood and watched them till he could bear it no longer.

He was turning to leave the box, when a young man entered with outstretched hand and cordial greeting.

" 'Pon my word, Clinton, I'm delighted to see you back. I shall be quite a lion to-morrow for having been the first to shake hands with you. I hope you don't mean to leave town soon. You're come just as the season is pleasantest. Quantities of pretty girls this year, and one superb! There she is opposite, Miss DeKahn. Isn't she superb! Cold as an icicle though! We call her la bella ~~Ghiaccinola~~. If you'll believe it, she won't waltz, or polk, or dance any of those dances! But in spite of that, she's immensely admired. She's *the* belle, in short. — It won't do to say a word about her haughty ways before the girls, though. It puts them in a rage. They declare, one and all, that she is the gentlest, sweetest creature in existence. All I can say is that we men don't find her so. I thought she had no more heart than a mill-stone, but Charley Prevost lately seems to have found the way to please her. He's always with her. People say they're engaged. I suppose it will be out soon. That's he behind her now. You know him. — By George, what a smile! I don't wonder Charley's dead in love. He's wild about her. — What, you're going?"

Mr. Clinton rose. He turned one instant as the opening door sent the blaze of the gas-light without full on his face. Handsome Charley's eye rested upon his friend. He sprang to his feet.

"By Jove! there's Clinton just going. I must catch him. Good-night. I shall bring the new photographs to-morrow." And the door closed behind him.

A heavy blow seemed to fall upon Lilian's head as he spoke and hurried from the box. What! Mr. Clinton had been near her, opposite her, and she had not seen him! Perhaps he was coming to speak to her. — Her heart shook her whole frame. She could hardly draw her breath. She waited, she listened, every nerve strained to its utmost. The moments passed. He came not. — And at that very moment he was somewhere. Charley Prevost was talking to him, looking at him, seeing him. — And she! — bound there to her seat, with the lamps glaring before her, the din of the orchestra in her ears, the obtrusive voice of the singer vexing her sense! — She could not endure it, — she could not stay. She would go. She would hurry. Perhaps she should pass by him in the corridors. Only to see him! —to see him once more!

With quick, glancing eye and feverish step she passed along the half-deserted passages, void of the form she longed to look on. Down the broad staircase, through the empty hall, into her carriage. — She had looked in vain.

The world seemed an aching tomb. She spoke no word. She reached her home, her own room, and walked up and down the long night through.

—◆—

XXXI.

DAYLIGHT was streaming through the half-opened shutters when Lilian entered her grandmother's room, and stood beside the bed. The grandmother started as she caught sight of her darling's hard, dry eyes and parched lips.

"Good Heavens, child, what is the matter! And you haven't been in bed all night!"

Lilian took her grandmother's hand in hers, knelt beside the bed, and looked supplicatingly in her face.

"Grandmamma, do you love me?".

" Love you, child ! I love you better than any-thing in all the world. What is it, my darling? Tell me, tell your grandmother."

" Grandmamma, take me home. I can't stay here. Take me home at once, to-day, — only let me get away from here, — take me home ! "

And Lilian buried her face in the bedclothes and sobbed, but shed no tears.

" Did I ever refuse you anything, my pet, my darling, my own dear child?" said the poor old lady, quite overcome with sympathy for Lilian's unaccountable distress. " You shall go whenever you please, you shall go to-day if you like ; only don't sob so, my darling, don't, — it breaks my heart." And her grandmother drew Lilian's head towards her and kissed her many times.

Lilian had never loved her so much as at that moment.

And how had Mr. Clinton passed that night?

Handsome Charley had met him in the vesti-bule, had accompanied him to his hotel, had sat with him till two in the morning.

What had handsome Charley said? " You see, Clinton, I want to tell you all about it. You're the only one I can, for all the nice fellows in our set are in love with her themselves. And I know you won't think me soft, nor call me a fool." And Charley had launched out into a detail of all Lilian's perfections, and had confided to his friend all his love for her. The young man was thoroughly in earnest.

" I tell you, Clinton, it's enough to make a man good, just to look at her. Sometimes when I'm talking with her, she fixes her eyes upon me, and they look so pure that I feel ready to shoot myself when I remember some things; — and you know I've not been half so fast as most of the fellows here. I know I should never have a wrong thought again, if she'd only marry me. And, do you know, though I dare say I seem like a conceited ass to say so, I've great hopes she will ! One thing's certain to start with, — she doesn't care for any one else, and that's a great thing you know, — and then she is certainly kinder to me than she is to any of the rest. You can't imagine how her manner has changed during the last few weeks. She used to seem to think it as much of a bore when I talked to her as when any of the others did, and now she smiles when she sees me, and she lets me talk to her by the hour together. She shakes hands with me,

—she doesn't do that to any other man in town. It looks as if she liked me, doesn't it?" and Mr. Clinton was obliged to confess that it did.

But as he looked at the handsome, high-spirited, affectionate youth, he thought bitterly how little he was able to appreciate the woman he loved. He thought of all Lilian was and of all that she might be. Such a marriage seemed impossible. It was like assisting at the preparations for her funeral.

"But you were travelling all last night. You look tired. I must be boring you to death," said handsome Charley at last, and he took his leave.

Mr. Clinton sat down, leaned his elbows on the table and buried his face in his hands.

He had seen her again, more beautiful than ever. The sight had roused his emotions to their highest pitch. He loved her to desperation. He, the strong, self-governed man was utterly helpless before this passion. She *must* belong to him!— She *must* be his!— Could nothing make her love him!— He smiled in derision at the thought. He was almost old enough to be her father. What chance had he beside young, handsome Charley!

He had been weak in coming; — his brow flushed as he accused himself of weakness. He would see her no more. He would leave the city immediately. He would go, he knew not where, — anywhere save where she might be. He must bear it as he could. He was not the only sufferer in the world. God knew what the torture was. He who had made man's heart so to love woman could measure what he had to endure. There must be some good in it. God knew. And the end must come!

And his thoughts wandered into higher regions among the eternal hills, bright with the red light of a fadeless morning. And the sharp pangs faded, and the fiery torment slackened, and with steadfast eyes he looked up into the brightening sky, and saw the opening day.

Mr. Clinton threw himself down and slept, slept long, for he was weary. He knew not how long, when handsome Charley burst into the room. Was that handsome Charley?

The bitterness of death was on his face. He threw his hat across the floor, cast himself into a chair, and covered his face with his hands.

"Oh, Clinton, I'm the greatest wretch on earth. — She won't have me!" And the poor young fellow gave a despairing sob. "I don't know what to think. I don't know what to make of it. I felt so sure. It's all so strange.

" I went there this morning. The trunks were standing in the hall all packed. I asked for her. They said she was engaged. I sent in my name, and she said she would see me. I went into the drawing-room, and there she stood, all white. She said, ' You must bid me good-by. I leave town in an hour.' Then I don't know what I said except that I loved her and begged her to marry me. She trembled all over and sat down as if she couldn't stand. I went on and told her how I loved the very ground under her feet, and how I knew she could make me anything she chose ; and then she gave a great choking gasp and burst into tears. I begged her to answer me, to say just one word, and she looked up as if she were begging me not to kill her, and said, ' Oh, don't ask me ! ' — Then I knew it was all over with me. I wished I were dead, and I said so. Then she whispered out that she was afraid she had been very much to blame, that God knew she did not mean to do wrong ; and then I begged her to say that I might have some hope. I went down on my knees to her. I asked her to give me just one little hope. Then she looked

at me in a way that I shall remember to my dying day, and said, 'I have done great wrong. I
will atone so far as I can. I can give you no
hope. I love another.' She turned crimson, then
white. She looked like death. — Then I was
going. There was nothing more to be said. She
came up and held out her hand and asked me to
forgive her. I tried to bid God bless her, but I
couldn't speak. — Then I went out and have been
wandering for hours till I came here. But I can't
stay. I'm too wretched to stay anywhere. I
came to you for I knew you'd feel for me. And
I wanted to tell it once. Now I shall never speak
her name again. I'm off to Europe to-morrow.
Good-by, Clinton."

He wrung his hand and was gone.

Mr. Clinton's heart seemed beating all over
him. "She loved another!" He dared not
think of what he hoped. She had left the city.
He would follow her. He looked at his watch.
He had slept long. It was too late to take the
train. He would drive out. He could reach his
house that night. He could see her in the morning.

An hour later he was on his way.

It was a warm evening in early spring. The bursting leaf-buds filled the air with sweetness. The stars were so bright that they lighted the whole landscape. An indescribable softness, like hope ripening to fruition, filled the air. The winter was over; the spring was come. A still rapture of delight breathed around. The silent thanksgiving of Nature reëchoed from Mr. Clinton's heart. From his innermost soul he thanked God.

It was late ere he reached his home, but he had no wish to sleep. He threw open the glass doors that opened on the lawn, dismissed the servants, and sat down to think. Thought was now a pleasure too precious to be lost in sleep.

All was still when on his ear there came a sound, the bounding footsteps of a dog. Up the lawn it coursed; into the room it dashed, and Great Heart crouched before him with a piteous whine. He ran to the glass door, then back to Mr. Clinton, howling all the while. — Had harm come to Lilian !

Mr. Clinton sprang down the lawn guided by the flying hound, towards the church, into the graveyard, past her parents' graves. The dog disappeared within the circle of cypresses that shaded Mira's grave.

There on the marble stone lay Lilian. He lifted her in his arms. She was insensible. The great drops stood on his brow. He felt what had brought her there. It was love of him that had led her in despair to the grave of the woman he had loved. He groaned aloud as he thought what she must have suffered ere the power of endurance had deserted her. He clasped her to his bosom. He called her by her name. He pressed warm kisses on her lips, and shivered as he felt how cold they were. What was he to do ? He could not take her to her home. It was too far. He must carry her to his own. Through his distress darted a flash of joy.

XXXII.

LILIAN knew not how long she lay insensible. She slowly unclosed her eyes. Circling clouds of mist surrounded her. She saw every object as at immeasurable distance. An aromatic odor filled the air. A soft light fell from a lamp above her. She lay as in a pleasant trance. The vapors rolled by degrees away. Objects seemed approaching her. They had a familiar yet half-forgotten aspect. Her eyes rested on a veiled picture, then on a figure before her. It looked like Mr. Clinton. But where was she? Had she not gone and knelt by Mira's grave? This was not the gravestone. She lay on a silken couch. Where was she!

Her senses returned in full vividness. She recognized the room, — the room wherein she had tended Mr. Clinton, years ago, — unseen since then. She fixed her eyes upon the figure before her. It was he! With a cry, she started to her feet. She wavered. She was falling. He caught her in his arms, and replaced her on the couch. Lilian burst into tears. She wept violently. Mr. Clinton walked up and down the room, in silence, casting agitated glances upon her. At length her tears ceased. He approached her. He bent over her. He fixed his eyes upon hers, with a long, deep gaze. It needed no words. She knew that he loved her. That long mysterious gaze! That silent ecstasy! He bent lower, as drawn by an invisible force; cold trembling lips were pressed to hers, and Mr. Clinton sank on his knee, while the heavy beating of his heart shook the couch whereon she lay.

She lay in peace. Her trouble was ended. She had entered into her rest. She floated on a golden sea. God above her, — her lover beside her. She was at peace.

From the far distance of the ocean, nearer and nearer, came a moaning sound. Closer and closer it drew, wailing like a soul in pain. A sudden gust shook the house, the casement was burst open, and the chill night wind swept across the room, and lifted the veil that hid the picture on the wall. The lamp flared fitfully, as Mira's sad eyes looked down upon the lovers. The silent lips moved; but Lilian and Mr. Clinton heard nothing, saw nothing, felt nothing, save that they loved each other; and, with long, sobbing sighs, slowly, reluctantly, the wind retreated as it came.

Mr. Clinton rose from his knee. He staggered. The room reeled around him. He passed his hand across his forehead. With a powerful effort, he compelled himself to be calm.

His movement broke the spell that had bound Lilian. She half rose, and said, in her clear, steady voice, —

"I must go."

" Yes," he answered ; but you are not strong enough yet. Wait."

He brought her some rich cordial.

" Drink."

She obeyed.

He lifted her from the couch. He placed her upon her feet. He steadied her steps. He led her to the glass door, and they passed out into the night. But the glory which needs not the sun was around them ; a light brighter than that of day rested upon them. To them there was no more night.

XXXIII.

And the registry of the little church below the hill bore a new record : —

" Married, — Harvey Clinton to Lilian De-Kahn."

XXXIV.

LILIAN entered the library, where her husband sat reading. He laid down his book, and smiled as she advanced. She seated herself on his knee. She smoothed his cheek. With taper fingers, she raised the heavy locks from his brow.

“ What is it, Lilian,” he said.

She laid her hands on his shoulders. She bent in her head, and fixed her eyes earnestly upon him.

“ I want to go to the prairies. I am too happy to live in houses. I want to be where the earth is broader, the sky higher,—where all is fresh and free. I want to ride wild horses, and sleep in a tent. I can’t bear any longer calls, visiting, dress-ing, dinner-parties, and all those things. I want to be in the far West, alone with you.”

Mr. Clinton’s eyes kindled. Did that beautiful creature wish to leave civilization for those savage wilds, that she might be the freer to love him? He caught her to him, and kissed her passionately.

“ We will go,” he said.

--◆--

XXXV.

Lilian stood beside her husband, and looked across the wilderness of troubled waters of the mighty flood.

Fast they had sped, across broad inland seas whence the eye vainly sought the shore; past deafening torrents thundering from sky to earth, shaking the solid ground; over endless plains dotted with peaceful herds; through mushroom cities sprung up in one night, filled with restless crowds, the hum of traffic and the din of trade; along wide-swelling rivers teeming with floating life;—from the populous, law-loving East to the wild luxuriant West, the land of giant growth of Nature and man,—the land where Luxury and Barbarism walk side by side, where Peace and Order are replaced by Violence and Lawless Will. And still they sped onward towards the still wilder West, to the home of the Indian and the bison,—to the green prairies, rolling like a pathless sea, to break at the foot of the great mountains.

—◆—

XXXVI.

AND, at last, the long journey had reached its end. Lilian had her heart's desire. She was alone with him. Illimitable as his love the green earth stretched before her; deep as his tenderness the blue sky arched above her, trembling with its own intensity; soft as his protecting care the white clouds glided by, casting broad shadows to shield the prairie from the fervid sun.

Each circling hour brought its own delight,
Glad was the bright day, glad the quiet night,

When rose the glorious sun in pomp of pride,
With rosy pennons flaunting far and wide,
Chasing the timid stars that shrank away,
And cowered out of sight before the day;
Forth from her snowy tent the lady came,
Greeting, with upturned brow, the Heart of Flame.
On her fleet steed the lover placed his bride,
And o'er the glittering prairie, side by side,
Dashing apart the flowers, bespecked with dew,
Fast, as the birds that soared above, they flew;
Careering o'er the bending, rippling grass,
Startling the plover and the grouse they pass.
Wild snort the steeds; with shrill and joyous neigh,
They chase their shortening shadows, as the day
Waxes apace.   Then o'er the boundless plain,
Rolling beneath the fresh breeze like the main,
Towards the distant, snowy tent again,
Their rapid way they take.
When the white sun glares fiercely from the sky,
And fainting in the heat the prairies lie,
Beneath the shade of overhanging trees,
Resting her husband's head upon her knees;
Listening the ripple of the little stream,
That rises, falls, like music in a dream;
Culling the blossoms springing 'neath her hand,
Weaving their bright hues in a flowery band;
Watching the bison on the distant lea,
That pass like dark hulls on a verdant sea;
Noting the gorgeous hues and outlines strange,
Of the wild butterflies, that fearless range,
Flitting around, and resting on her head,
With quick and quivering pulsation spread
Their jewelled wings, — she sits, nor hardly knows
Whether she wakes or sleeps, so deep is that repose.

And when the sun sinks burning to his rest,
Pressing his brow into the cool, fresh breast
Of the sweet earth, then would they wander forth,
Their only guide one clear star in the north;
And, far from sight of their wild hunter guard,
Would send their souls and voices heavenward,
In swelling harmonies of soft linked song.
Or, as with woven arms they paced along,
Beneath the large, bright stars, their speech would fall
Upon their love, that boundless All in All,
That swallowed up all else.   Then to their tent,
With many a lingering pause, their steps they bent,
Pausing to gaze on the white mist that rose
Its curtain round the sleeping plain to close;
Pausing to list the last, faint, lingering note,
That died on the still air, from the far throat
Of some half-sleeping songster. Towards the blaze
Of the bright watch-fire they come. They raise
The yielding portal of their dwelling light.
They enter, side by side. The loving night
Receives them, loving, — hides them from our sight.

———◆———

XXXVII.

WEEK followed week, but brought no weariness to Lilian. She knew the flight of time only by the waxing and waning of the moon, as it rose, night after night, the only moving thing in those unbroken solitudes. Day by day they wandered on, across level plains, enamelled with countless flowers, beautiful and new; over prairies rolling in endless waves as though a solid ocean had been arrested in its heaving; through savage ravines, crowned with rough battlements of rock; beside gentle rivers, sweeping under wooded banks; past milk-white torrents, raving down their stony beds;—farther and farther from the haunts of men they journeyed on in fulness of content.

They had come to a rushing stream, clear and pure, bordered by leaning willows which laid their green fingers on the water as though to stay it in its onward course. They pitched their tent, for the horses' heads were drooping, and the sun was high overhead. The hunters departed on their daily search for game. Mr. Clinton and Lilian remained alone beside the crystal water. Its ripples seemed to beckon them onward; its murmur seemed to bid them follow. They yielded to the influence, and sauntered under the grateful shade, following the moving cadence of the cool, fast-flowing river. Pleasant it was to walk where it might be that no human foot had ever trodden before;—pleasant to listen to the song of the river, sung to their ears alone.

They passed under the flickering shadows until they came to where the banks narrowed and rose abruptly. A great willow had fallen across the stream, and rested its spreading head upon the opposite bank. The luring song had ceased. The water fretted and foamed below.

"Let us follow the river no longer," said Lilian.

. They crossed the slippery bridge. Beyond grew young willows and alder bushes. Through the close branches they saw the gleaming of some large white object. They broke their way through the belt of thick shrubs. An unexpected sight met their eyes. Before them, on the border of the prairie, stood one solitary Indian lodge. No sign of life was near it; — no horse, no dog, no fire. The white bison skins which covered it were carefully secured on every side as if to prevent entrance or egress. They came near and listened, — there was no sound. They called, — there was no reply.

Mr. Clinton cut the cords of deer sinew that fastened the closely-guarded entrance, and drew back the covering. The light fell dimly within. A cold tremor passed over Lilian. It was the home of Death.

Before them, on a low bier, lay a rigid form, plumed, painted, decked in gayly embroidered buffalo robes; — a warrior stricken in his prime. The tawny brow frowned terrible as in life. The sinewy arm that lay across his breast seemed ready to seize the tomahawk that lay beside his piled-up saddle, tent, shield, and spear. He looked as though he had not been dead an hour.

Awestruck, Lilian drew near and gazed upon the lowering face. A terrible attraction was in it that chained her to the spot. She had never before looked on the dead. That awful moment when we first make acquaintance with what all past have been, all to come shall be, was upon her. As she looked, a rush of thought bore her back to the quiet graveyard beside the little church. Again she stood beside two long, narrow, grass-grown graves. Great tears gathered in her eyes and fell heavily. They brought her back. She was again in the lonely lodge on the prairie, the dead warrior's face before her, with closed lids looking stonily upwards into hers. And that was Death? She saw it, — she would touch it. Slowly, shrinkingly, she raised her hand and laid it upon the frowning brow. A sudden cry escaped her. Was it the chill contact of mortality that brought it from her lips?

"It is not cold. He is not dead. He is alive!"

Mr. Clinton tore open the buffalo robe and bared the broad, scarred chest. No motion was perceptible. He held the bright blade of his hunting-knife to the warrior's lips. It grew dim.

"I will hurry to the tent for cordials. Are you afraid to stay here?"

"I will stay."

And Mr. Clinton entered the thicket that lined the river's brink, and left Lilian alone with the living dead.

She took the nerveless hand in hers and chafed it with her soft palms. She touched lightly once again the stern forehead. The life of the warrior grew momently more precious in her sight. She thought not of his ferocious life, of his murderous past. She felt only that he was a human being, — a fellow-man. She breathed warm breath upon his closed eyelids. She chafed again his hands. — Suddenly she started and fixed her eyes intently upon his face. A slight shiver passed over the prostrate form, another and another. Slowly the black line of the meeting lids unclosed, and the savage looked on her.

Terror rushed upon her, urging her to fly. Charity, more powerful, held her to her post.

With trembling touch she continued to chafe the hand she held.   It warmed fast in hers.

With fascinated look she watched the snake-like eye fixed immovably upon her, listening the while with straining ear for the sound of her husband's return.   A rustling in the willows, — a step ; it was he.

" Ha, this is well," said Mr. Clinton as he entered the lodge ; and he looked upon Lilian with his rare, brilliant smile.   She was repaid.

He cut apart the covering of the lodge and gave admittance to the light and air.   He gave to him the cordial he had brought.   It quickened the flow of returning life.   The Indian sat up, struck his hands together, and said some words in harsh guttural tones.

Mr. Clinton signed his ignorance.   The warrior stretched forth his knotted arm, took the white hand,' pressed it to his heart, then laid it upon his head.

The willows again parted, and forth from their green covert strode the hunters.   With practised eye they had followed the trail which led from the deserted camp.   As their look fell upon the scene before them, they drew back and spoke hurriedly and excitedly to one another.   Lilian went towards them.

"We found this Indian left as dead. He was in a trance. We have brought him to life."

"It's a great pity you did, Madame," answered the old French half-breed who was the chief of the party. "It's Wild Cat's life you've been saving. He's the blood-thirstiest scoundrel on the prairies. The whites did him a harm once: burned his lodge with his squaw in it, and he's hunted them like wild beasts ever since. He'd have dashed your brains out with his tomahawk just now, if he'd been strong enough to hold it. If you'd just allow me, I'll finish him this minute, and it will be good riddance to the prairies." And he raised his rifle menacingly.

Lilian threw herself before him. "Put down your gun. No one shall harm him," she said authoritatively; but it was with some trepidation that she returned to her husband's side and re-peated what she had just heard.

"I know something of Indian character," re-plied Mr. Clinton. "I am willing to trust him, although I have no doubt that Baptiste's account of him may be true."

The warrior had watched with keen interest the dialogue in which he was so deeply interested. He saw the hostile gesture of the hunter and the protecting movement of Lilian. His face betrayed no emotion, but his small, bright eye noted every change on the faces around him. He knew that he had twice owed his life to Lilian.

How would he repay her?

———◆———

XXXVIII.

Lilian and Mr. Clinton issued from their tent the next morning as the sun was rising. The sky was covered with small, fleecy, silvery clouds, through which the light broke softly over the dark green of the plain. The indescribable happy stir of awakening life filled the dewy air. The shrill cry of the plover came from the distance. On the summit of the steep cliffs which advanced on one side, leaped and frisked the snowy ahsahtahs, rejoicing in the first beams of the sun.

Below, by the side of the stream, the hunters were assembled around the fire, preparing their morning meal, while ever and anon a short, dry laugh would mingle with their talk. They appeared to have forgotten the unwelcome presence of Wild Cat.

He sat on the ground at a little distance from

them, his knees drawn up, his chin resting upon them, his eyes moodily fixed upon the ground.

" Faut obèir á Madame," said the old hunter, and he offered the Indian a portion of their fare.

He silently refused it.

" What's the matter, Baptiste, won't he eat ? " said Mr. Clinton, advancing towards the hunters.

" No, Sieur, — he wouldn't eat yesterday, and he won't eat to-day."

" What's the reason ? "

" Who can say ? "

" You know the language of his tribe ; ask him."

The Indian had raised his head, and was watching the flight of two eagles that were circling in broad sweeps high over the prairie. As the hunter addressed him he muttered a few harsh syllables and returned to his former position, his head resting upon his knees.

" He says, Sieur, that he had rather be free in the Spirit land than live a captive in this. He means to starve himself to death, it seems, — the best thing he can do, to my mind, the murdering rascal ! " And an expression of heartfelt disgust came over Baptiste's bronze-green face.

" Tell him that he is free," said Mr. Clinton.

Unwillingly the hunter obeyed.

The effect of the words upon the savage was electrical. He sprang to his feet and stood towering erect, his face and form of stone converted into quivering nerve and muscle. He extended his arms as if to embrace his newly-found freedom. He looked up to the sailing eagles and saluted them with his hand. Suddenly his face changed, he crossed his arms upon his chest and sank his head upon his bosom.

" He has no horse," exclaimed Baptiste in answer to Mr. Clinton's inquiring look ; — " that's it. A man on the prairies without a horse isn't a man, — he's just nothing but food for the wolves. We've only horses enough for ourselves, but we are in the country of the mustangs. We shall fall in with a troop before long, and then he can catch one for himself. I shall be glad to see him out of the camp, since Madame won't allow us to make an end of him as he deserves," added Baptiste in an injured tone, as he turned to the brave and spoke again in Indian tongue.

XXXIX.

THE sun was pouring down the intolerable fervor of his noontide rays. Hunter, horse, bird, and plain, were deep-drowned in the mid-day siesta. The only sound, the only motion, came from the cool, fast-flowing river. One only object braved the fierceness of the heat. Erect on the cliff, where the ahsahtahs had sported, stood the warrior, his plumed head and flowing robe sharply defined against the deep blue sky. The varied colors of his raiment glowed in the sunlight. He was bathed in the fiery rays. Shading his eyes with his hand of bronze, he looked towards the horizon. Hour after hour he stood. Horses and men awoke, stretched themselves, arose; the birds again took up their song; the coolness of declining day replaced the scorching noon; but still the warrior stood, shading his eyes with his hand of bronze, scanning the distant horizon.

As the sun reached its lower level, the brave bent eagerly forward; raised both hands to his forehead and gazed still more intently, then turned, sprang down the cliffs, and hastened to the camp. In a few moments, mounted on a powerful steed, armed with a long, coiled lasso, he was speeding towards the south.

The party stood watching his onward course.

Far in the distance of the prairie they saw a small, dark cloud. It rapidly approached, growing each moment larger. The Indian threw himself on his side and rode towards it, hidden behind his horse. Fast the dark cloud advanced, changing its aspect as it came nearer. They could distinguish the varied colors — chestnut, white, black, and pied—of the small, round-bodied prairie horses. Their long manes and tails flowed behind them, as they curvetted, plunged and pranced in their playful course. Fearless, they approached the solitary horse with his hidden rider, speeding to meet them. They came towards him, whinnying as if to invite him to join their joyous company. As the foremost advanced with outstretched necks and quivering nostrils, the warrior sprang erect with a shrill cry, the lasso was launched, and the running noose fastened around the neck of the nearest of the band.

Wildly neighing, snorting in affright, their heels thrown high in the air, their long tails streaming, the drove confusedly wheeled and dashed thundering back to the remotest verge of the prairie. The sound of their rushing hoofs and shrill neighing lessened, died ; — they were gone. Gone, all but the captive, who, rearing, plunging, his eyes flashing, his nostrils smoking, his lips frothing, vainly struggled to break free from the choking lasso. Skilfully the Indian alternately checked and loosened the cord, now allowing his prisoner to bound forward at full speed, now throwing him back on his haunches. The sweat poured from the reeking sides of the frightened, furious animal. He was white with foam. His strength began to fail. He stood trembling in every limb, then, stiffening himself for one final effort, he collected his sinking forces for a piercing scream, as if to call his companions to his aid, and fell heavily on his side.

The Indian dismounted and approached his prisoner, carefully keeping the cord tightly stretched. He cautiously advanced to the head of the prostrate animal. He stooped and tightly grasped his nostrils. The mustang struggled more faintly. He breathed into them. The struggles ceased. The wild horse lay as though dead. The brave passed the cord several times around his lower jaw and raised the captive's head. The animal obeyed unresistingly. The warrior mounted his horse and returned leading his submissive prize, his happy freedom ended, his glad liberty lost, — a cowed, unloving slave.

XL.

THE next morning as Mr. Clinton left his tent, Baptiste came to meet him with a moody face.

" Wild Cat's off, Sieur, — off with all his traps. He slipped away in the night. It's my opinion he means us no good, and if you'll take my advice, you'll hurry up the river and get out of this region as fast as you can. I don't like his slipping off in that way. Great pity Madame didn't let me shoot him! " And Baptiste raised his rifle, his inseparable companion, and let it fall heavily on the butt end.

" Qu'est ce qu'il y a, Baptiste ? " said Lilian, coming forward.

" Le chat Sauvage s'est sauvé, Madame, voilà tout." And Baptiste returned to the hunters, who with unwonted activity were making their preparations for an immediate departure.

Internally grateful to Baptiste for his reticence, Mr. Clinton placed Lilian on her horse so soon as the tent was struck and the pack-horses laden. Warily they rode forward, keeping close to each other, talking little, laughing not at all. Cautiously they scanned every rock, tree, cliff, and ravine which they passed ; but no trail, no scout, no hostile sign of any sort presented itself. At the end of the third day, any lurking alarm that Mr. Clinton might have felt was dissipated; and laying aside his recent precautions he resumed his customary walks and rides with Lilian, who in spite of his efforts to conceal their uneasiness, had been somewhat disquieted by the air of sinister apprehension of the party.

They had travelled far up the course of the river, — for water was too scarce on the prairies to be willingly forsaken, — and had arrived on a high plateau, surrounded by volcanic peaks, which shut in the plain with an irregular barrier of turreted walls, giant bastions, and frowning towers. The herbage was scanty and bitter, the air thin and sharp.

" What a dismal place," said Lilian. " It looks beleaguered by hostile fortresses. Let us turn back to-morrow."

And she retired from the gloomy prospect so soon as her tent was pitched; and, tired by the day's journey, lay down and fell asleep. She was roused by Mr. Clinton's voice, —

" Lilian, come hither."

She hastened to his side.

The large, full moon was slowly rising over the distant battlements of rock, pouring a flood of silver light over the plateau. What had been the barrenness of desolation, touched by those rays, now smiled in pathetic beauty. Sweetly solemn lay the landscape before them, tempting them forth. They left the camp, — the peacefully-grazing horses, the hunters lounging and chatting around the crackling fire, — and strayed across the plateau. They wandered long. The scene was too peaceful, too beautiful to leave. They knew not how far they had gone, when they perceived that the moon was sinking. They turned to retrace their steps, but the distance was greater than they had thought. The moon sank, and darkness covered the plain; but the watch-fire shone brightly in the distance, guiding them homeward. It was growing larger as they advanced, when Mr. Clinton stopped abruptly, and laid his hand tightly on Lilian's arm.

"Hush!"

At the same instant she felt the earth tremble.

"Down!" he whispered, and he threw his arm round her, and bore her to the ground beside him. A rush swept by them, — a rush of horses' hoofs. It swept towards the watch-fire. The trampling died in the distance. Lilian had scarcely time to ask herself what she dreaded, when a yell so horrible, so unearthly, rent the midnight air, that she cowered into her husband's arms, and hid her face in his bosom. Again and again it came, mingled with the sharp report of fire-arms. Then all was still. She raised her head and looked. The watch-fire burned faint and fainter. It died out. Again the trampling hoofs rushed past, and in greater number than before. Again the sound vanished in the distance, and Lilian and her husband were alone,—— alone in the wilderness, alone, save the corpses by the watch-fire.

Was it for this that she had drawn him to the wilds? Had she brought him there to die? She wrung her hands in self-accusing anguish.

" O God, forgive me! God forgive me! I am the cause. — I!"

She fell on the ground whence they had risen. She grovelled at his feet. She embraced his knees, with harsh gasps.

He did not speak to her. He did not attempt to console her with words. He raised her. He seated himself on the earth, and took her in his arms. He soothed her as if she had been a little child; then, as she grew calmer, he spoke.

"Lilian, look upward."

She looked and saw the eternal stars,— God's handwriting on the celestial wall.

They gazed upward in silence together. They felt the Eternal Presence embrace them with its boundless love. Life grew as a very little thing, as they contemplated the majesty of Infinity. Lilian's soul drew in strength; and when her husband again spoke,— "O God, eternal Father, we are in Thy hands, whether we live or die: Thy will be done," — her keenest agony was over. She could say, —

"Amen."

The dark hours wore on. Wearied out, Lilian slept in Mr. Clinton's arms. He wrapped his coat about her, to protect her from the chill air, and, holding her close to his breast, watched through the night.

As the first glimmer of light broke above the gloomy barrier of the plain, he roused her. It smote him with a sense of cruelty to awaken her to all that returning day would bring; but their only possible safety lay in immediate flight. She awoke;— she stood up. Consciousness had lasted through her sleep. She waked to the full memory of all that had occurred, and with her husband's words of faith still sounding in her ears. She gazed around on the bleak, desolate plain. She lifted her eyes to him and smiled. At least they were together. He caught her to his heart. A spasm sharper than that of death wrung it. She smiled; and she had wakened to her first day of starvation.

They sought the river, to descend unseen its wooded banks. Their best chance of meeting travellers lay in keeping close to the stream; and where else should they find water? They came to where the shore bore fresh marks of footsteps and the recent print of hoofs. They were close to the camp of the evening before. What was there now?

"Stay here while I go forward." And seating Lilian on the bank, Mr. Clinton went towards the silent spot. In a few moments he returned. She rose and gazed at him eagerly. He shook his head.

"We must hurry forward as fast as your strength allows. The body of an Indian is there also. They will return to seek it."

They hastened down the shore of the fast-flowing river. With feverish speed, Lilian pressed on, insensible to hunger or fatigue, until the plateau,

with its gloomy battlements and frowning towers,
lay behind them; and, passing-through the narrow
gorge down which the river rushed foaming, they
entered on the illimitable prairie beyond. Then
her strength forsook her all at once. The sun
was high. She had walked since daybreak, fast-
ing.

Mr. Clinton laid her under the shadow of a
tree, gathered grass for a pillow to her head,
brought water in his hands for her to drink, and,
then leaving her, sought for wild fruits or berries
to allay the hunger whose pangs he also felt; but
not for himself. It was impossible that, amid that
profusion of flowers, under those magnificent trees,
on that rich plain, no food could be found, — no
berries, no roots. He searched on every bush,
beneath every tuft of grass, he tore up each
strange plant by the root, ever and anon returning
to look upon Lilian's pale face.

She lay quite still, apparently in a quiet sleep.
Through her closed lids she saw that his hands
were empty. She feigned slumber to lessen his
distress. Again and again he departed on his
quest. At last he came, fast hurrying. Did he
bring food! She sat up, she tried to rise to meet
him. Was it food! He poured crimson buffalo

berries into her lap. He threw himself down beside her. He kissed her over and over again. He bade her eat.

Scanty, insufficient as was the meal, yet it stilled their hunger for a while, and gave Lilian strength to go on — on — in the desperate hope of meeting help where help was none, — on, day after day, until that last hope died away.

Lilian suffered less than Mr. Clinton. She rested upon him as a child upon its mother. She had not lived long enough to be over fond of life; and, as is usual with the young, she had little fear of death. If they must die, at least they would die together. Death was a small thing compared with separation. To die, — to be together forever in an union even more perfect than that of earth! It was not so greatly to be dreaded. They might have much to endure first, — her courage wellnigh failed her at the thought of his suffering, — but it would be only for a little while, and then they would be together in Eternity. And she raised her face, serene and fearless, and thanked God.

And Mr. Clinton, how did he look upon the lingering death that seemed inevitable for both?

Existence was to him a precious thing. He

knew its value better than did Lilian.   The love
of life was strong in his powerful brain, his full
veins, his vigorous frame.   But for her, — for
Lilian, — there lay the bitterness of death.   Day
by day, to see her young life wasting; hour by
hour, to watch her slow decay ; and at last to lay
her down in the wilderness to die !   How could
he bear it ?

He called up all his forces.   He braced himself
for the struggle.   He strove with his anguish ; he
mastered it.   It was —— therefore it was right.
The bitterness passed ; and, from the height of
submission to God's will, he looked down undis-
mayed upon the Valley of the Shadow of Death.

They had set forth in the flush of joy, hope,
and love.   Nothing remained to them now, save
love.   The pitiless prairie stretched before them,
gay, luxuriant, beautiful.   The red antelopes
sprang rejoicing by in graceful bounds, the
brown buffaloes darkened the plains, the white
ahsahtahs frolicked on inaccessible cliffs.   Birds
innumerable filled the air with song.   All was
glad and smiling around them.   Nature refused
her care to them alone.   Each day saw their steps
slower, their faces more wan.   They smiled on

each other from their hollow eyes, but their parched lips rarely parted.

At length their bare and scanty food failed utterly. Not a berry, not a root, rewarded Mr. Clinton's search. Lilian could go no farther. A torpor of mind and body stole over her, benumbing the insufferable torment of her hunger. Objects grew small and dim before her sight. She tried to speak. Her tongue lay immovable. Her husband spoke to her. Her ear was deaf. Scarcely knowing why he did so, he bent down a tall sapling, and tied his handkerchief to its topmost branch, then returned to watch those last moments which were to take her from him but for a little while.

Mercifully the extremity of his sufferings of body and mind had blunted his sensibility to pain. The last had come, and he sat calmly by his dying wife. He sat holding her hand, looking upon her ashen face. He saw nothing, save that wasted form.

" Hallo ! "

He gave no heed. It was but another of the mocking delusions that had tormented him during those days of misery now past by.

Nearer again.

" Halloo ! "

Mr. Clinton turned his head. A figure was
spurring over the plain, — a white man! Too
late! she was dying. And he fastened his eyes
again on that motionless form.

The horseman galloped up.

" God Almighty! Why, you're starving, ben't
you ? " And the old leather-skinned, weather-
beaten trapper knelt beside Lilian, while Mr.
Clinton sat, with dull eyes, dumb and immovable.

" She'll come to," exclaimed the trapper, springing to his feet ; " but she's precious near gone,
and you are, too," he added, looking attentively
at Mr. Clinton. " Do you hear," he repeated,
raising his voice, " she may come to again ; be
alive ; do you understand ? "

A look of intelligence shone from the heavy,
hollow orbs ; a spasm of returning animation
passed over the impassive face. Mr. Clinton rose,
staggering, and leaned over his wife.

The trapper hurried back, with a leathern cup
in his hand.

" Here, jist you lift her head, if you can, and
help me pour this down her throat."

They raised the light, — ah, how light! — form.
The brandy was poured within the thin blue lips,

slowly, drop by drop. Would she, could she swallow? Mr. Clinton watched the emaciated throat. There was a moment of agonized suspense, then a faint movement, another, — she swallowed! The husband burst into tears and sobbed aloud:

"Come, now," said the trapper, encouragingly, — "but 'ta'n't no wonder." And his own voice grew thick. "There now, lay her down; she must rest before we give her any more; — and you jist drink this yourself. You need it e'en a'most as much. Now I shall be spry and make a fire, and have some broth in no time. That's the proper vittles for her, pretty dear. I swunnys!" And shaking his head in comprehensive protest, the old trapper set rapidly about the preparation of the food that was to save them.

Cautiously they administered it, drop by drop, spoonful by spoonful, with many a rest, many an anxious pause, ere Lilian gave other sign of returning life than that evinced by the act of swallowing. At length her eyes languidly opened. They were glazed no longer. Mr. Clinton bent over her.

"Lilian, we are saved!"

A slight, almost imperceptible motion of the fingers he held was the answer. She had heard.

" Now jist as quick as she's a leetle brighter, I shall go off down to the camp," said the trapper. " There's a party of us, you see, about four or five miles off, that's all; and I'll bring up a wagon and put her in it and take her down, and the trappers' wives will nurse her up first-rate. Precious lucky I came along, though — there wasn't much life left in her. I always did kinder believe in Providence ! "

And he galloped away.

The stimulus of his presence removed, a drowsiness came over Mr. Clinton. Lilian still lay to all appearance unconscious. He sat beside her motionless, sometimes vaguely wondering why he did not feel more glad, then once more relapsing into partial insensibility.

He was aroused by the cracking of whips, the rattling of wheels, and the shouts of drivers. Up the plain came a great white-covered wagon, drawn by a long team of mules. The trapper galloped to his side.

" Come, rouse up ! We're moving the camp up here. We thought she couldn't stand being carried so far, — and here are the women come ahead to take care of her," he added, as the lumbering wagon drew up and a bevy of young gayly-dressed

Indian women sprang from it and crowded around Lilian, their dark beauty, and full, rounded limbs, contrasting painfully with her death-like pallor and shrunken form.

With many a pitying ejaculation they tenderly raised her in their arms, and bore her to the bed of soft mats they had spread for her in the wagon. As she was placed upon the rude couch, Lilian opened her eyes and looked uneasily around. The youngest of the band caught the distressed glance, nodded intelligently, and darted away. In a moment she returned bringing Mr. Clinton.

As Lilian's eyes, still restlessly wandering, fell on his face, the shadow of a smile hovered over her wasted features. She feebly opened her arms. He fell beside her and buried his face in her bosom.

The Indian women softly withdrew, and left them, who had been as the dead, and were alive again, alone to that first silent, tearful rapture of thanksgiving.

XLI.

THE camp was pitched for a long halt; the wagons corralled in a circle, and chained together

so as to form a sort of fort in case of attack from
the Indians ; and, leaving a strong guard, the trappers departed, taking with them their pack-mules
laden with all best calculated to tempt the cupidity
of their savage customers. They were less ad-
venturous than usual, for the Indians were in an
aggressive mood, and Mr. Clinton's party was
not the only one that had been recently attacked.

"I don't think Wild Cat had anything to do
with that ere skrimmage," said the old trapper,
one of the guard left behind, to Mr. Clinton,
" coz, you see, the tribe around that plateau and
his'n are allers a-fightin'. He'd be much likelier
round in these diggins," — and he cast a searching glance around the peaceful horizon. Nothing
moving was to be seen save one great eagle circling in the upper air. As they watched him, he
rose high, poised himself, then swooped upon his
prey.

The care and skill, the affectionate devotion of
her Indian nurses, the healthful food, the quiet
sleep, and most of all, the sense of comparative
security, soon brought back the roundness to Lilian's figure, the color to her cheek. She rallied

more quickly in every way than did Mr. Clinton;
her sympathetic nature reflected more vividly
than his what was around. Now that the cup of
the wine of life was again held to her lips, she
drank joyously of it. No shadow from the past
troubled its sparkling depths, no recent bitterness
lingered on its brim.

But with his reflective, tenacious nature it was
not so. His past entered into and became a part
of himself. He could not free himself from it, he
could not shake it off. Its presence haunted, oppressed him. Long after the light had returned
to Lilian's eyes, the elasticity to her step, he
would sit wearily leaning back, watching her
as, lying under the leafy shadow of the great
trees, she petted and played with a little antelope
brought home to her by one of the hunters; or,
surrounded by the Indian women, her fair cheek
and snowy hands glowing like tinted alabaster
beside their tawny beauty, she wiled away the
time learning to embroider deerskin shirts and
moccasons with gayly-dyed porcupine quills, or to
weave pliant mats with brightly-tinted rushes,
whilst the smiling circle with language of rapid
signs, explained, corrected, and admired. He
would sit watching her with a careworn look, as

if he dreaded to see her snatched from him, and felt his inability to protect her. Had she not already nearly died before his sight while he stood powerless by! Could he but again see her in the safety of her distant home he could be at ease. — Never till then.

——◆——

XLII.

At last the trappers returned, laden with furry treasure. The camp broke up, and moved eastward. The long line of white wagons with the file of heavily laden mules, the patient led horses, the mounted trappers in their fantastic garb of embroidered deerskin, now and then dashing off for some tempting shot at a stray buffalo or antelope, rolled together over the plains ; now fording rivers on rudely constructed rafts, now striking through broad belts of woodland, now steering across the open seas of green, now winding among interlocking ravines, till the nightfall stopped their onward march. Then by some wooded spring or river bank, the halt was made. Around lay the prairie half-hidden in the twilight, above rose the tall waving wreaths of smoke, while below blazed the quickly-kindled fire, its bright light reflected by the encircling wall of white wagons, and glancing on the sun-browned faces and half-savage garb of the trappers as they hastened to and fro, picketing the horses, unlading the mules, and suspending the product of the day's hunting upon rude wooden props before the mighty blaze, while the Indian women, with their black hair hanging in carefully braided tresses over their bosoms, their long ear-rings and gaudy necklaces, their particolored skirts and brilliant kerchiefs, their little feet and dainty ankles encased in richly embroidered moccasons, stood in the dancing firelight, chatting and jesting in happy immunity from the lot of hard labor to which their less favored sisters in Indian lodges were doomed. It was a gay and cheery sight. And long after the evening meal was over, and Lilian and Mr. Clinton had retired to the wagon which had been assigned them by their hospitable hosts, they would hear the sound of laughter, song, and story, with which the hardy trappers beguiled the early night, while from time to time the laughter of the Indian women, as they chatted apart, would rise like the bubbling of an unseen brook.

XLIII.

IT was the mid-day halt. The wagons stood here and there beneath the shade of the huge trees which grew beside the course of a little stream. The mules unladen, rolled luxuriously in the soft thick grass. The horses stood knee-deep in the water, drinking long draughts, ever and anon raising their streaming nostrils and gazing approvingly around. The Indian women were busily preparing the grouse and plover which were to form the delicacies of the coming meal, while those of the trappers not busy with the animals were gathering dry wood for the fire.

Lilian and Mr. Clinton were the only unoccupied members of the party. They strolled towards a small eminence which rose abruptly near, — a rocky islet on the turf. They climbed it to enjoy the full sweep of the prospect. They gazed delightedly on the landscape, the gently-winding little river, the wooded ridge that rose midway in the plain, on whose green carpet scattered herds of buffaloes were peacefully grazing, when Lilian said eagerly, —

" There must be another party near us. Do you see that smoke ? "

Mr. Clinton looked where she pointed. A pale blue line writhed upward above the tree-tops of the ridge. He looked keenly around. Smoke was rising from more points than one. He lifted Lilian in his arms and bounded down the rocks.

"Run for your life," he said, as they reached the ground. He shouted aloud as they sprang forwards, —

"The Indians."

In an instant all was breathless haste. The wagons were corralled; the horses and mules driven into the circle; rifles, guns and pistols, primed and loaded; bowie-knives and daggers thrust in the belts, and bags of powder and shot placed open at hand.

As the hasty preparations for defence were completed, and the trappers took their places lining the wagons, while their wives crouched behind them, herds of buffaloes came galloping over the ridge and confusedly rushing over the plain.

"They're coming," said the old trapper who stood beside Mr. Clinton.

"Harvey, you say I must not have a gun," said Lilian, standing beside him with blanched cheeks and flashing eyes, "but at. least I can load for you."

" Yes, that you can," said the old trapper, " as well as any of 'em. That's the women's part of the bis'ness. Gives us a great advantage, you see. But here they are, — now for it ! "

As he spoke the Indians issued from the wood and came pouring towards them in a long, waving line, with streaming pennons and flaunting robes. Their spear-heads and gun-barrels glittered brightly in the sun, as, bending low on their horses' necks, they dashed forwards.

" Don't look out. Stand back and keep below the line of the woodwork," said Mr. Clinton.

Lilian obeyed and knelt, grasping the powder-horn, ready to serve him. She could see nothing without, she knew not how far the foe had advanced, when before, behind, on every side, rose the vengeful, bloodthirsty yell that she had heard at midnight on the plateau. As it shook the air, a storm of whistling arrows and hissing balls hailed on the wagons. It was answered by a sharp, rattling volley. The fight had begun.

Lilian could distinguish nothing. She heard on every side a sharp, continuous rattle mixed with oaths and shouts, and howling above all the fearful warwhoop. The air was white with smoke. She could but dimly see the forms of her husband

and the trappers. Dexterously she fulfilled her task. Her eyelid did not quiver nor her hand tremble, as she poured the black grains, and dropped the death-dealing bullets in rapid succession into the quickly returning weapons.

The tumult raged more and more furious. The horses and mules plunged madly within the circle. The wagons heaved as the terrified animals, snorting and screaming, tore round their narrow bounds, seeking to escape. It was one deafening din, when Mr. Clinton, dropping his gun, staggered backwards and fell on his side. The old trapper strode across him and took his place.

Lilian threw down the powder-flask, and flung herself on her knees. She tore open his shirt. A pulsing crimson stream was flowing from his side. She vainly sought to stanch it, unmindful of the raging storm around, when suddenly a yell, louder and wilder than any which had gone before, rose close to her ears. The trappers sprang from the end of the wagon into the inner circle, as the covering was ripped open, and yelling, whooping, demon-like, the savages leaped down beside her. She saw a crowd of dark, distorted faces, a confusion of uplifted arms, the glitter of tomahawks and the shining of knives. A hand was twisted in her hair. She was borne backwards. She gave one look upward. A terrible form stooped over her with upraised arm. She closed her eyes. The blow — where was it ! — She felt herself snatched up. She saw herself lowered into the arms of a painted savage. The warrior who first seized her, lifted Mr. Clinton in his arms and sprang with him to the ground beside her amid the surging crowd of upturned, yelling faces.

The firing, the war-whoops, the confusion, were smothered in the thick, black veil of unconsciousness that descended upon Lilian. She knew no more.

----♦----

XLIV.

LILIAN was recalled to her senses by the rush of air upon her face. She felt herself tightly clasped and rapidly borne forward. Half benumbed by terror she unclosed her eyes. She was on a horse, an Indian's arm was cast around her, another horse was flying forward by her side. Bound to its back, extended at full length, lay Mr. Clinton. The Indian held both bridles. On they dashed. The grass flowed beneath them like an emerald river. The trees looked misty as they passed. The air whistled in her ears. Lilian's brain whirled. She closed her eyes and tried to pray. No words would come. Her thoughts mixed with the unremitting muffled beat of the horses' hoofs, the whistling of the wind, and the iron pressure of the Indian's arm.

She knew not how long their course had lasted when the horses stopped. The Indian sprang to the ground, lifted her down and placed her upon her feet. She tried to advance towards her husband, but her limbs failed under her and she sank on the grass.

A belt of young willows, a solitary lodge on the edge of the prairie, were swimming before her giddy sight. Timorously she glanced at the warrior. Wild Cat stood before her. " Life for life ! "

—◆—

XLV.

THE sentinel stood at his post on the lonely Western fort. He looked over the sad, bleak prairies, lately so smiling. The setting sunlight lay sorrowfully over their tawny expanse. He watched the sun go down, the mists rise and the shadows fall. As he stood and watched, over the yellow plain, half-veiled in the spectral mist, half hid in the cheating shadow, he saw three mounted forms appear as if they had risen out of the earth, one an Indian. He rubbed his eyes and looked. Three!—there were but two riding towards the fort. The Indian had disappeared. He had vanished into the shadow. He had melted into the mist. He was gone!

XLVI.

THE gun had sounded. The last farewells had been spoken, the last handkerchiefs had fluttered from the stern of the steamer. The crowd on the pier had dispersed, the passengers had sought their state-rooms to put their possessions in what order they might before the coming crisis. The great ship steamed proudly down the wide-opening bay, passing innumerable smaller, white-sailed craft and crowded ferry-boats, that shouted and cheered her on her outward way. The wind came freshly from the ocean, the vessel caught the motion of the waves. Lilian and Mr. Clinton stood together at the prow. His eye brightened and his color rose as he breathed in long draughts of the invigorating air.

As the voyage proceeded, the languor which had hung over him ever since the summer, vanished. His figure rose erect and stately as before. The grave smile returned to his eyes, the deep cadence to his voice.

Seated on the gallery by the great wheels with Lilian by his side, he passed his days, now reading to her, now watching the ceaseless variety of water and sky, now looking down with her upon the unending comedy of the decks below. Like the shades cast from a magic lantern, the motley crowd passed before them : — a pretty danseuse with brilliant eyes, a small foot and modest manners, from whom all the lady passengers shrank with abhorrence, and who held in solitary state a much frequented court of gentlemen on the upper end of the promenade deck ; a little wizened, hungry-eyed man, her father, who was never seen to speak to her ; thirty German Jews, shading from dirty black to dirty yellow, all thin, all small, all in shaggy great-coats and plaided waistcoats ; a returning French minister, politely bored with everything and everybody, with himself most of all ; a rich, portly merchant, with his faded, sickly wife, five naughty boys, the torment of the whole company, whose principal diversions consisted in slid-

ing on the deck across the line of promenaders,
and in giving to their mother and the other nervous ladies in the saloon, fictitious accounts of ice
ahead, mutinies among the stokers, fires just dis-
covered in the hold, leaks rapidly gaining head-
way, and passengers crushed in the machinery;
whilst their eldest sister, a hard-featured girl of
sixteen with a premature sense of responsibility,
wasted her existence in the fruitless attempt to
make her brothers behave like little gentlemen;
a fair-haired American, always ill at sea, who
had linked her fate to that of a French travel-
ling-agent, compelled by his occupation to make
incessant voyages, and who moaningly followed
her lord over the world like a sick spaniel; an
anxious mother with a family of young daughters
and a strong-minded governess with short black
curls and an elastic step, who practised her Italian in conversation with the wife of a Genoese
macaroni-maker, returning crestfallen from an
unsuccessful attempt to establish a *succursale* in
America, when not engaged in supervising the
eldest daughter, a blonde of seventeen with regular features, regular movements, and regular
expression, whose only recreation consisted in
walking up and down that part of the deck most

directly under mamma's and the governess' joint observation, when any daring youth offered his arm for the promenade; while the second daughter, a brunette, with full, quiet lips, watchful eyes and broad forehead, was devouring in secret " By- ron " and " George Sand," which she had smug- gled on board in her capacious travelling-bag ; and the third daughter, a beautiful little gypsy of eight, was set aside as "nothing but a child," and left free to receive the adoration of the gentlemen in general, when not occupied with the danseuse; a knot of fast young men, weak-kneed, mottle-faced, with very tight French boots and very loose Eng- lish coats and trousers, voting America slow, and bound for the hells, *coulisses,* and *bal masqués* of Paris ; a blear-eyed banker, worn out with the care of his own and other people's money, haunt- ed by alternate fears of beggary and of softening of the brain ; wonderful women from the far Southwest, who breakfasted in flounced silks and gold bracelets, and changed their dress five times a day, escorted by dark, roughly-attired men whose sole occupation consisted in smoking and betting. Old and young, rich and poor, re- fined and vulgar, sick and well, all mixed together in involuntary contact and unwilling intercourse,

a menagerie of human beings with but one feeling
in unison, the desire to reach the end of the voyage.

———◆———

XLVII.

THE sky was gray. The wind rushed across
the shining, neutral-tinted white-crested waves,
and howled and lamented amid the rigging. The
vessel rolled and pitched heavily with straining
engines and slowly-revolving wheels. The promenaders one after another gave up their unsteady
occupation and retreated below, or sat dismally
on the wet settees looking round in vain for a
break in the sullen uniformity of the leaden sky.
A few ladies wrapped in heavy cloaks and hoods
still braved the drizzling rain. The danseuse,
surrounded by a group of water-proof admirers,
maintained her accustomed place at the end of
the deck. As the drops grew larger and heav-
ier, she reluctantly arose to seek the shelter of the
saloon. Refusing the offered arms of her attend-
ants, she made her way along the slippery deck.
A heavy wave struck the vessel, — it lurched
violently. The girl fell, and was dashed against
a settee. A piercing scream mingled with the

rattling revolution of the great wheel as it hung suspended high out of the water. As the vessel righted the gentlemen pressed around the danseuse.

"Ah ne me touchez pas, ne me touchez pas, pour l'amour de Dieu," she shrieked as they sought to raise her.

"Yes, do see what's the matter with the poor thing," said Lilian anxiously, as Mr. Clinton rose from the settee beside her.

He mingled an instant with the group, then hastily descended the cabin-stairs. He returned with the surgeon. The group grew larger. Smothered cries came from its midst, then it opened and several men precipitated themselves down the stairway. Mr. Clinton came back to Lilian.

"The poor girl's hip is dislocated. They are going to bring a mattress and take her down to the saloon to set it there."

"May I?" asked Lilian, rising quickly.

"Yes, it would be kind." And Mr. Clinton gave his arm and led his wife towards the group which opened deferentially at her approach.

On the wet deck lay the half-fainting girl. Lilian knelt beside her with gentle, pitying words.

The danseuse opened her eyes and looked up wonderingly for a moment, then with a groan, closed them again.

· The mattress was brought. Shrinking and moaning the girl was carefully lifted upon it, carried down the narrow stairs into the great saloon and laid upon the table. The company rose *en masse.* The lamps already lighted shone brightly down upon the girl's pallid face and black clustering hair which, disarranged by her fall, fell loose over her shoulders.

" Passengers will be so good as to leave the saloon," said the surgeon, looking around. In a moment the great room was deserted save by those in immediate attendance upon the sufferer.

As the company retired, the stooping, hungry-eyed old father entered and came hobbling up the saloon.

" Ah, la pauvre mignonne ! " he whined as he reached the group around the table.

The girl's lids suddenly lifted. She launched at him a look of hate, and turned her head away.

" Now," said the surgeon, " if you, Madam, on one side, and you, stewardess, on the other, will hold her hands tightly, we are ready to begin."

As the girl felt the hands around tighten on

her shoulders and limbs, she fixed her affrighted eyes on Lilian's face.

"Oh don't let them kill" — a prolonged shriek filled out the sentence. There was a dull sound, and the surgeon raised his head and tossed back his hair. A deep groan followed the shriek. The girl had fainted away.

"Nothing to be alarmed at, Madam," said the surgeon to Lilian, who looked almost as pale as the sufferer. "Patients often faint under it. It's a rather severe operation. We had better get her into her state-room before she comes to."

The insensible form was carried away, the old father following, whining, "pauvre mignonne!"

In a few minutes the stewardess returned.

"I know it's too much to ask, ma'am, but I can't undress her alone, and none of the other ladies would come near her if I asked them. If you would be so very kind."

Lilian preceded her to the state-room. As she turned the handle she heard a harsh, rasping voice within.

"Fille maudite!"

She entered. The creeping old father stood beside the child.

"Ah ça, chérie, ça va mieux, n'est ce pas?"

The girl's cheeks were flushed. A look of defiance was on her face.

"Madame est mille fois trop aimable." And, with a cringing salutation, the old man left the room.

Carefully they cut apart and removed the girl's clothing. As they came to the inner garments, they perceived a narrow belt of sackcloth sewed firmly around her waist. Wondering, Lilian was preparing to cut it open, when the girl hastily prevented her.

"Ah no, Madame. I promised my mother always to wear it."

Still more surprised, for she had never thought of danseuses as people that had any mothers, Lilian continued her offices till the girl was disrobed, the surgeon again summoned, and the injured limb arranged as comfortably as circumstances would permit.

"May the Holy Virgin reward you, Madame," said the danseuse fervently, as Lilian bade her good-night.

She rejoined Mr. Clinton with whom the surgeon was conversing.

"Yes, a most unfortunate thing. She will have a great deal to suffer for want of proper care. The stewardess can't give her the necessary attention, it's impossible."

" What care is necessary ? " asked Lilian.

" There's nothing more to be done for the leg at present, of course, but she ought to have some one by her the whole time to tend her and nurse her. But there's a patient waiting for me. I must go. One of those five boys will be quiet for some time to come. He's eaten himself ill. I've a great mind to keep him in his berth till we land."

And the surgeon bowed himself off.

Lilian repeated to Mr. Clinton all that she had heard and seen in the danseuse's state-room.

" I never before supposed that any of those people could be respectable, but there is something about that girl that interests me very much," and she paused thoughtfully ; then as one coming to a sudden determination, she looked up with pleading eyes. " It is dreadful to think of her suffering for want of proper attention during these next few days ! If you were willing I should be so glad to take care of her ! " And she watched his face.

It was some moments before Mr. Clinton answered ; at length, —

“ You shall do as you wish,” he replied. And, to the measureless astonishment of all on board, Mrs. Clinton took her place as the sick nurse of the danseuse.

“ The girl can’t be like danseuses in general,” said the world of the steamer. “ The Clintons must know something about her respectability, or so very fastidious a person as Mr. Clinton would never allow his wife to be with her a moment. Very kind of Mrs. Clinton, certainly. I think I shall send and ask how the girl is to-day.”

XLVIII.

During the first days of Lilian’s attendance, her charge maintained an invincible reserve. She seemed overwhelmed with constraint. Lilian would sometimes catch her eye fastened wistfully upon her, but it was immediately averted.

At length the girl broke silence. Lilian was standing at her feet, rubbing the benumbed and aching limb. She looked up and met the wistful gaze. She smiled encouragingly. The smile seemed to unlock the girl’s lips.

“ Ah, Madame,” she exclaimed, “ if I could tell you how I thank you ! You do my heart as much good with your gentle looks as you do my poor leg with your soft hands. It is years since any one has looked on me with anything but contempt. It has crushed me into the dust. And yet what wrong thing have I done?" she spoke hurriedly and excitedly. "Is it my fault that I was forced on to the stage, that I am dragged over the world from one city to another by that wretch, my father? Ah, Madame, if you only knew how wretched I am, and how happy I was with my mother, — Oh, my mother, my mother!" And the girl burst into a passion of tears.

Lilian, much moved, attempted to console her.

"Oh let me cry. It does me good. It is so long since I have shed a tear." And she wept long and freely.

"Would it distress you to tell me about yourself?" said Lilian, when the girl was calmer.

"Oh no, Madame," she replied gratefully. "It would be a comfort to me. I am so lonely. I should like to feel that there was one person in the world who knew how unhappy I am.

"My mother was the *femme de chambre* to an old lady in Paris. I was brought up in a convent till I was twelve. I was happy there. The nuns were very kind to me. They used to give me pictures of the little Jesus, and ask me if I should not like to be his little bride. I had a picture of Saint Catherine, being married to the little Jesus, hanging up in my room. They told me that the world was a dreadful place, and that if I left the convent I should have to work hard all my life, and that I should most likely grieve the little Jesus so that he would love me no more, and that I should never go to heaven. So I told my mother once, when she came to see me, that I had made up my mind that I wanted to stay in the convent and be a nun. Two or three days after that she came back and took me away. I was very sorry, and the nuns were very angry. I cried, but they comforted me by telling me that when I was older I could come back and be a nun, whether my mother liked it or not.

"My mother took me to the old lady's house. I found that she had told her that she must leave her service and take a room where she could have me with her. The old lady said that she could not let her go away, and that she might bring me there, only I must be very quiet and make no noise.

" When we arrived at the house, my mother

took me through a great many rooms into a large, gloomy chamber where the old lady lay in bed. The bed had great high posts and was hung with faded tapestry. There was a black crucifix with an ivory Christ hanging by the head of the bed. The old lady's face was just the yellow color of the Christ, and she had great black eyes that looked me through. I was afraid of them, and hung behind my mother. She led me forward to kiss the old lady's hand, and she told her how grateful I was. Then she led me away, and I never saw the old lady again.

" I was kept all day long in a room looking out into a court-yard, and I had a great deal of sewing given me to do. It was a large, bare room lined with wardrobes in which the linen was kept. There was a table before one of the windows, and two chairs. It was very dismal. My mother was all day long in the old lady's room, and I had nobody to speak to. I used to cry and wish myself back at the convent twenty times a day. My only diversion was in looking out of the window. On the opposite side of the court-yard was a long row of windows that lighted a great hall. It was a dancing-hall. I used to climb upon the table before the window and watch the master giving his lessons. There were a great many pupils, and it used to amuse me very much to see them moving all in time, though I could not hear the music. There was one pretty little girl of about my own age. I watched her most of all. I wished I could know her and talk to her. I became quite fond of her by looking at her so much. I wanted to be like her. I used to arrange my hair as she did hers. I tried to do the exercises that she did. They seemed to bring me nearer to her. I grew to like them very much. I became very supple and strong. I used to dance half the time, but I sewed all the faster when I did sew, and always had my work finished by evening. At last I could do all the exercises better than the little girl I liked, better than all the rest. I could throw my foot higher, turn on my toe longer, and bound farther, than any of the pupils. I practised in that way a great many months, but nobody knew how I spent my time.

" At length the old lady died, and my mother took a little room, and we used to sew together from morning till night. Then, how happy I was ! I learned how good my mother was. I loved her with my whole heart. All the week we used to sew for the shops, but on Sundays she used to take me to mass, and after that we used to walk together. She always bought me a bouquet of violets on Sundays. I used to look forward to it all through the week.

"We lived in that way till I was fifteen. I was tall of my age. My mother never sent me out alone. But one day she was ill, and I was obliged to carry home our work to the shop. When I came home I found my mother weeping. The little clock, the only ornament of the room, was gone. The door of the wardrobe was open and the things scattered over the floor. I said, "Don't cry, mamma, I will run for the *sergents de ville.*" She shook her head. She couldn't speak at first. At length she sobbed out, ' Oh, my child, no one can help us, nothing can be done. It is your father.' I never knew I had a father till then. He had taken all our little savings, and was gone !

"We changed our lodgings and tried to hide ourselves. We only went out after dark. Our pleasant walks on Sundays were ended. We lived in constant fear at first, but a long time passed, no one came to trouble us, and we began to feel more secure, and even to venture out by daylight sometimes.

"One Sunday morning my mother had gone to

15

buy something for our dinner. I was feeling very
happy, the sun shone so brightly and my little
bird sang so loud, and I began to dance in the
middle of the room. I had made a long pirouette
and was standing on one toe, the other foot higher
than my head, when I caught sight of a gray head
with hungry cunning eyes peeping in at the door.
I was dreadfully frightened, and ran to shut it,
but the man pushed it open and came towards
me with his hands stretched out, saying, 'Em-
brasse moi, ma petite.' I screamed and ran into
the corner. 'Comment donc, tu ne veux point
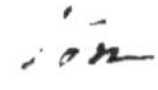 embrasser bon père ?' he said. I looked at him
with horror, such, — such as I feel for him now.
He sat down, looked at me from head to foot, and
said, nodding his head at me, 'Tu danses joli-
ment bien. Avec toi je saurai bien me tirer d'em-
barras.' I grew more frightened every moment.
I heard my mother coming up the stairs. I was
running to the door, but he got up and stood in
the way. 'Ah, te v'là,' he said, as she came in.
She let her basket fall and sat down on the chair
next her. 'Don't be frightened,' he said, grinning at her, 'I haven't come to take your money.
I've come to take her,' and he pointed at me. I
gave a scream and ran into my mother's arms.

' Now there's no use in distressing yourselves and acting a tragedy,' he said. ' That's girl's worth a great deal of money to me and I mean to have her.' ' What are you going to do with her ? ' said my mother, holding me close. ' Put her on the stage, to be sure,' he replied. All we could say or do was of no use. He carried me off to a theatre. I had to dance before a great, coarse, fat man. When I had finished he said I should do very well with a few lessons, and my father signed some papers and received some money. My mother and I cried all that day. The next morning my father came and took me to the theatre. I found myself among such girls as I did not know existed. I heard such language that I was ready to sink into the ground. They were all jealous of me because I danced better than they did. Only the mistress was kind to me and said that I should do her honor. When I went home I told my father that I would not go again without my mother. He said she should not go there. Then I would not eat. I fainted away at the third lesson, and my father had to give in and my mother went with me. After some weeks I made my début. They put on me a dress which was cut half way down to my waist and came up

above my knees.   When my mother looked at me
she cried worse than ever.   The woman came to
rouge me, but she said I did not need any.   My
cheeks were burning, I was so ashamed.   I was
to dance a *pas seul.*   The curtain drew up and,
I saw a great pink wall of faces before me.   I
was so frightened that I could not move.   The
music began three times.   The people pitied me
I suppose, for they applauded me a great deal.
That gave me courage.   I danced, and they applauded me more and threw me bouquets.   When
I came off the stage I ran into my mother's arms
and hid my face in her neck.   I felt as if I should
die of shame to have danced in that dress before
all those people.   It was only the beginning.   I
have danced so ever since.

After my début the other danseuses were more
disagreeable than ever, but I had my mother and
I did not care.   A great many gentlemen came
and spoke to me in the *coulisses,* as I sat beside
my mother, but I would never look up or answer
them.   I hated it all.

My father did not give us any of the money I
earned, and my mother had to work very hard,
for my lessons and rehearsals and performances
took up so much of my time that I could help

her but little. I think he tried to make her work herself to death that he might be free of her. I hated him, — Mon Dieu, how I hated him, how I hate him now!" And she clinched her hands. "He had his wish. My mother grew weaker and weaker. At length she died. Before she died, one day she begged me always to wear this belt of sackcloth round my waist to remember the blessed Jesus by, and she said it would also every morning and evening remind me of her, praying for me in heaven. So she sewed it on, — she was so weak that she could hardly hold the needle, — and I have worn it ever since. A few days after, she died. The night she died my father made me dance.

"After that we went to Italy, and I danced in the great cities. The public was pleased with me, and we began to live at large hotels. I used to drive about in a carriage, and I had a maid. A great many gentlemen came to our apartments, but I used to lock myself up in my room, and think of my mother, and cry.

"One night I came from the theatre. My maid who slept in my room when I was wakeful or restless, was not waiting to undress me. My father told me that she was ill, and had gone to bed. I went into my room and locked the door. On the table stood the bread and wine and water that I used always to take before I went to bed. I put the wine and water to my lips. It had a bitter taste. I held the glass up to the light. There was a white powder in the bottom. I remembered how coaxing my father's tone had been when he told me to go in and eat my supper. I began to feel afraid, yet I knew he could not want to poison me while I gained money for him. I felt imprisoned. I wanted to get out of the room. I threw a great black silk mantle over my shoulders so that passers-by should not notice my dress, unfastened the shutters, opened the long window, and stepped out upon the balcony. I stayed there a long time, it was so fresh and quiet after the heated, crowded theatre, and the noise of the music and applause. I stood leaning on the stone balustrade; then I began to walk up and down. My satin shoes made no noise. As I passed my father's room I heard voices. The shutters within were closed, but a chink was left open. An impulse led me to look in. Before the table sat my father and a tall red-faced man, — a great nobleman who sent me flowers every day and letters that I never opened.

I had promised my mother never to read any such letters. I put my ear to the crack of the window. I heard, — I cannot tell you what I heard. For a moment I could not move. The tall man rose. The motion brought back my strength. I flung myself over the balcony, it was on the first story, suspended myself by my hands, and dropped into the street below. I ran, I knew not where. My only idea was to get as far away as possible. It was long past midnight, the streets were almost deserted, but, as I passed a turning, a party of young men caught sight of me. They shouted and pursued me. I ran like the wind. I turned a corner and came upon a line of carriages. The coachmen were asleep upon their boxes. I opened one softly, got in, shut the door and crouched down on the floor. I heard the young men run past, laughing and hallooing. I stayed there all night. Every time I heard a step I feared it was some one coming to look for me. All night I thought what I could do. At length I made up my mind that there was no law to protect me from my father, and that I must protect myself. When the day came I went back to the hotel. My father was out. I stood up and waited for him to return.

When he came home I told him that I would not
live, unless I could continue to respect myself.   I
told him that I was desperate, and so I was.   I felt
all the blood in my body singing in my ears as I
spoke to him.   I began to think I had better kill
myself at once to make sure.   He was frightened.
He apologized, he entreated my forgiveness, he took
the most solemn oaths never again to offend me in
any way ; he cringed before me.   How I loathed
him !   But he has not dared to break his word.

"Since then I have been in many cities, always
applauded, always despised, always miserable.   In
two years I shall be of age ; then I shall dance
no more, and, thanks to this accident, it will be
long before I can dance again.   It will free me
from my two next engagements.

"Oh, Madame, you cannot imagine what a life
it is !   To have no friend, — to be a slave.   Well
or ill, weary or strong, it makes no difference, I.
must dance just the same.   And the exercises are
so fatiguing, that I have to go through.   A danseuse cannot skip a single day, else she must prac-
tice double the next.   And the dreadful women
I am obliged to meet.   It makes me feel as if I
were wicked myself.   I feel so old already.   It is
only two years since my mother died, and I feel

as if it were twenty. And then the crowds of gentlemen who come around me; the speeches they make to me. Oh, Madame, you do not know how cruel men are!" And the girl buried her face in her hands.

Lilian was painfully interested. Were there really no means of rescuing the girl from such a position, of saving her from the hands of such a father?

"How are you, my angel?" whined a voice at the door, and the old, gray-headed father peered in. The girl impatiently turned her head to the wall, and, with a cringing bow, the head disappeared.

When Lilian joined her husband for her evening walk, she found a young man, of open, manly bearing, deeply engaged in conversation with him. He broke off what he was saying, bowed low, and retired, as she took Mr. Clinton's arm.

"I have been hearing a love-story," he said. "That young man is, to all appearance, seriously in love with your charge. He has never seen her on the stage. He has fallen in love with her on the passage. He is from the West. He says that he has more money than he wants, and no near relations to interfere with him, and he has made up his mind to marry her, if she will have him."

" Then he has not yet offered himself."

" He can find no opportunity. He does not choose to apply to her father; he says that he never has a chance to speak to her alone, and that she sends back his letters unopened. I fancy that he desires you to sound her inclinations."

" It would be the happiest thing in the world for her !" And Lilian related the girl's story to her husband. " Tell him to send another letter to-morrow when I am with her, and I will see that she reads it."

As Lilian sat the next morning in the narrow state-room, the stewardess appeared with a letter in her hand.

" Take it back," said the girl, angrily, as it was handed to her.

Lilian took it from the stewardess and broke the seal. The girl gazed at her in mute astonishment, as she quietly read it through.

" There is nothing here that your mother would not wish you to see," she said, as she finished it. " Read it," and she gave the letter into the. girl's hands, and left her alone.

When she returned, the traces of tears were on the danseuse's cheek. She was preoccupied and anxious, and spoke no more.

The silence was broken by a hurried rush, a cry, " Land ! "

Lilian started to her feet, and met Mr. Clinton at the door. They joined the crowd on deck. The sunlight fell gayly on the animated groups. Smiles beamed on every face. Joyous laughter and exclamations of delight filled the air. One common sentiment of pleasure united for the moment the mass of human beings that thronged the decks, mounted the settees, clambered on the bulwarks, and stood up in the boats. All eyes were fixed on a low, dark line, the first glimpse of the Old World, that sight so deeply exciting to all denizens of the New. An unknown parent is about to receive them.

As they gaze, a new-born sentiment of love and gratitude swells within them. The Mother Country lies before them. Their hearts beat quick. Their eyes fill with tears. With faltering voice, they bid God bless her !

XLIX.

THE sun had set over the desolate waste of the Campagna. Vainly Lilian had strained her eyes for the first sight of the vast dome towards which they were pressing on. No golden cross caught the last rays of the sun, holding their bright promise high above the surrounding twilight. No majestic outline rose swelling heavenward, as if upborne by the great heart of human kind. The darkness came shroud-like down from the cloudy sky, and covered all before them with its impenetrable mystery.

Nearer and nearer to the unseen city they drew. Thicker and thicker grew the darkness. Whence it came she knew not, but a vague dread crept over Lilian. She sat closer to Mr. Clinton. She took his hand. She closed her eyes and strove to lose all sense of anything, save the touch that met hers.

A sudden shock, as they passed over some obstacle, threw her to the opposite side of the carriage. As she unclosed her eyes, they rested upon ghost-like, serried ranks of gigantic columns, planted in darkness, supporting darkness. A cold wind, as of the tomb, breathed from their recesses,

and brought the sound of rushing waters to her
ears. Did she fancy that it syllabled, " Return ?"
Was that a form, indistinct and misty, that glided
beneath the colonnade, waving them back ; or was
it but the flitting shadows moving as they passed
by ? Lilian's heart quivered. She grasped the
hand she held as if seeking protection against her
own imaginings.

Through long, dark, tortuous streets they passed.
At length, in a broad piazza, the horses halted.
The impatient beat of the hurrying hoofs, the im-
portunate rattle of the wheels ceased. As Mr.
Clinton lifted Lilian to the ground, through the
night and stillness mournfully sinking, came the
sound of a convent bell.

L.

THE morning sun shone upon Rome, the Silent
City, the City of Eternal Repose. Its countless
domes and cupolas rose against the dark blue of
the sky, their golden crosses glittering in the light.
The yellow moss upon the tiled roofs, the rich,
creamy stone walls of the buildings, basked life-
lessly in the warm rays. Motionless the white
clouds that flecked the deep azure above, hung

over the motionless city below. An atmosphere
of still decay, irresistible, unresisted, brooded over
all things. The sunlight, how heavy it was! It
weighed down that whereon it rested. The shadows, how black they were! They swallowed up
all whereon they fell. No sound pulsed through
the stirless air, save when, from time to time, the
long-drawn, melancholy cry of some itinerant
vender rose from the narrow streets; or some rude
cart, drawn by yoked buffaloes with heavy curved
horns, and lowering, savage eyes, or by gigantic,
patient, whitish-gray oxen, conducted by a swarthy contadino, would labor by. Silently the rare
passers glided along, like unreal figures. All
things seemed unreal to Lilian. She almost
doubted her own existence.

Seated beside Mr. Clinton, she drove through
the sad, silent streets towards the villa which was
to be their winter home. They passed ruined
palaces, whose stately façades and princely portals
contrasted harshly with their dismantled windows
and broken balconies, — deserted churches, peo-
pled by statues only, their open gates vainly in-
viting entrance, — fountains, whose changing torrents were the only things unchanged since the

great aqueducts first led their crystal streams away from their homes among the hills, — through grass-grown wastes, with here and there a capital, — an unformed heap of ruin, — by which golden-tinted children, with crimson lips and flashing eyes, played at the *morra*, as did of old their soldier sires in their camp before the barbarians, — while wrinkled beldames, seated on the ground, twirled the distaff, and watched the few scattered, browsing goats; past crumbling piles, — funereal monuments, — preaching their mournful homilies to the unrecking wind, which toyed the while with the wild flowers that stood triumphant where once armed men might vainly seek to win. And all was beautiful, — beautiful in its sadness, beautiful in its decay. A charm, faint, sorrowful, lingering, lay over all things, — the enchanted spell of Rome.

They drew up before a lofty old mansion, frowning in melancholy grandeur on the grass-grown street below. As the ponderous bronze knocker smote on the heavily-studded gates, arousing a host of clamorous echoes, they swung slowly open, and Mr. Clinton conducted Lilian into a broad, gloomy stone entrance hall. The iron-barred gates closed behind her with a jarring clash. Before her, on the opposite side of the hall, opened another ample portal, showing a vast garden beyond. Between her and its velvet sweeps of green, its rich luxuriance of perfumed flowers, its pleasant, silver-tinkling fountains, its grateful shade of stately spreading pines and bending trees, stood, glittering white in the sunlight, a richly-sculptured marble sarcophagus. A cold breath seemed to issue from it, and strike on Lilian's heart. And yet it was but an empty sarcophagus, richly wrought, glittering in the sunlight. The form it had enclosed, once tenderly deposited there with chanted prayers and solemn sacrifice, had melted into dust thousands of years gone by. The tears once shed over it had been dried ages ago. Long centuries had passed since the mourners who once surrounded it had gone into the land of shadows, wept in their turn by those who again had followed on the same spectral journey. It was a waif of the past, brought from its resting-place to ornament a garden. . What had it to do with her?

"The air here is too cold for you," said Mr. Clinton, as she paused with arrested step. "Come into the garden." He drew her on. "What a

magnificent sarcophagus! I never saw a finer."
And he led her close to it.

The figures which surrounded it were dancing
in gay revel. Youths crowned with ivy garlands,
maidens with floating robes, musicians with pipes
and flutes, all sculptured with lifelike energy.
As Lilian gazed upon it, the undefined dread
which had crept over her, died away. What was
there, in truth, to disquiet her? And yet, if she
turned her eyes from it, she shrank when she
looked back. She could reason away her uneasiness, but it lay in ambush, waiting till she was
off her guard, to return.

They turned from the empty marble shell, and
sauntered down the broad terrace which lay beneath the sunny southern wall of the building,
bordered by alternate orange-trees, with their
dark, shining leaves, and by old marble statues,
gray and time-stained. Here and there they
passed a jet of sparkling water, spouting from an
antique mask, and falling into a mossy basin, in
whose limpid cup gold and silver fishes swam glittering, in slow, unending circles. Little green
lizards, roused by unaccustomed steps, darted
across the gravelled path and flashed up the wall,
disappearing in some invisible crevice. Stately

peacocks watched them from ancient balustrades
of stone, and, at their approach, arched their purple throats, lifting their jewelled fans, resplendent
in the sunlight, and dropping their gleaming wings.
On the little lake, white swans, like silver images,
rested motionless, reflected on the unruffled surface
of the placid waters.

No breeze disturbed the foliage, no sound of
life obtruded on the ear. The gentle music of
falling waters seemed but to make the silence more
profound. All breathed a still, luxurious repose.
Lilian sighed with pleasure.

" Here I could dream my life away," she said.

" You are my dream," replied her husband, as
he placed her on an antique seat, and threw himself on the ground at her feet, looking up at her
face with eyes whose look of love was to her as
Heaven itself.

" And you will be happy here?" he half
queried, wishful again to hear her speak her
pleasure.

For all response, she bent and kissed his forehead. As she raised her head from the caress,
through the dark shining leaves, across the placid
waters, she caught the gleam of the white sarcophagus.

LI.

As the winter passed on, the undefined dread which from time to time swept over her was the only jarring string in the golden harp of Lilian's life. Her impressionable, emotional nature, stimulated by all around her, developed into new depth and richness. With interlaced arm, she stood beside her husband, on that wreck-strewn islet in the sea of time. Each wave, as it broke at their feet, brought to her ear a confused murmur of mighty names, mingled with distant battle-cries, with shouts of victory, with imprecations of down-trodden multitudes, with death groans of slaughtered hosts. On the dark waters of the mighty, all-engulfing ocean before them, rose the tower-girt marble city, with its House of Gold, its palaces of delights, its crystal waters, its pleasant gardens, its lofty porticos, its columned temples, its circling theatres, — all sculptured fair in the phantom light of fancy. Then, while she gazed, the spectral pile would sink, fall, crumble into nothingness, again to reappear, again to vanish, in ever-shifting variation. Nothing was stable, nothing secure on that changeful flood.

So, day by day, she mused among the ruins,

she pondered amid the shadows on the shore of
the past, learning the world's great lesson of the
unreality of material things,— the shortness of
life, the nothingness of time.

Her love borrowed a more poignant sweetness,
a sharper delight, a keener ecstasy, from the im-
pending shadow of Death and Desolation. The
sad luxury of sentiment and sensation, — which is
the breath of Italian existence, — penetrated her
whole being. A languid, delicious fragrance
breathed from her; her step became slower, her
motion more undulating, her voice lower, her eyes
more deeply luminous. A perpetual moonlight
seemed to rest upon her, sweeter than starlight,
softer than the sun.

Mr. Clinton felt, yet could hardly deplore the
change. True, Lilian's lips laughed no longer,
but never had their smile been so entrancing,
never had they so frequently sought his own.
Her eyes shone with a less brilliant radiance, but
in their liquid depths he saw his own image more
tenderly reflected. Her whole existence, softened
into pensive acquiescence, seemed melting into
his.

He had thought before that he loved her as

much as he was capable of loving, but now his feeling towards his wife deepened into painful intensity. His desire for her happiness was no longer a sentiment, it became a passion in itself. Her pleasure grew into the hourly study, the exclusive object of his life. All the stores of his varied knowledge were spread open before her; all the treasures of his artistic criticism unfolded to her; all the curious antiquarian lore he had gathered in his many travels displayed to interest her.

With gentle guidance, he led her through Rome's palaces of Art, — those treasure-houses of unimaginable beauty. A new, glorious world opened before her, — a world of repose, of majesty, of loveliness, awful, ineffable, — the world of Classic Art. And as she reverent stood and gazed, she felt all human passion, all shadow of grief, all memory of pain, sink into silence before the unapproachable sublimity, the divine grandeur, which fill those soundless temples. Stately they stand, and still, those ancient, godlike forms. A deathless life is in their nostrils, a changeless contemplation in their unswerving eyes. Empires have risen and fallen around their pedestals, ages have swept away the wreck of ages, the genera-

tions of men in countless succession have defiled
before them, yet still they stand serene, unmoved.
Their marble faces look down on us as erst on
the long-vanished masters of the world. The
strifes, the cares, the birth, the death of men con-
cern them not. Their life is not as ours, — they,
the Immortals of the earth.

With lingering, oft-returning step she passed
through pictured halls and storied fanes, wherein
the lives of great men have been wrought to
tapestry with thought the cold, bare walls. The
awful vision of Michael Angelo scowled at her
from the Sistine Chapel. The soft, bewitching
grace of Raphael smiled from the canvas, as she
stood entranced. On the sweet majesty of An-
drea, on the transparent lusciousness of Titian, on
the thoughtful grandeur of Domenichino, on the
pathetic sweetness of Guido, on the childlike
charm of Correggio, on the rich voluptuousness of
Paul Veronese, on the grave earnestness of Pous-
sin, on the learned refinement of Leonardo, on the
long succession of the masters of past times, she
gazed with ever new delight.

In those vast palaces, those dwellings of vanished state, rich with the spoils, filled with the
trophies of the past, she spent long hours of each

succeeding day, drinking in beauty as flowers
drink sunlight. All about them was delightful to
her; — their proud façades, conscious of fallen
estate, yet still holding a bold front against decay;
their ruined court-yards, grass-grown and paved
with broken stones; their slowly-trickling fountains, green with velvet moss; their rows of muti-
lated busts, sadly looking down from their open,
deserted galleries; their deeply-worn, broad, stone
staircases, ascending through half-obliterated fres-
coes to the widely-cracked, carved, and gilded
doors; their long vistas of silent halls, with their
once gayly-painted ceilings now toned to dim
shade; their marble floors, once trod by the stately
company whose fading portraits look down from
the walls; their ancient, black-spotted mirrors,
which reflected the pomp and pride of lighted festival, and whose tarnished surfaces now give back
but the outline of some chance stranger from
foreign lands. Into these desolate halls, beggared
of all save Art, she came each day, and gazed
and listened to the loving, learned voice beside
her, ever pointing new beauties to her quick, ap-
proving eye; ever leading her through the human
errors of execution up to the divinely-imparted
conception, — teaching, explaining, sympathizing

ever.   And Lilian listened, and learned, and loved.

As they drove over the mournful solitude of the Campagna, he would guide her to the sites of long-vanished cities, — a few green ridges and scattered bricks alone remaining to show where the first crimson footsteps of Rome's victorious march had been pressed, — and build again for her their walls and citadels, and tell her of their valiant captains, and their daring, desperate deeds, before they sank at last beneath the strokes of their indomitable, vindictive foe.

Leaving their carriage, they would wander over the sunny, desolate plain, here and there passing a broken column, a fragment of a statue, or some crushed pottery, — frail relics of long-buried household life, turned up by the lazy plough of some half-clad peasant, who stared in sullen silence as they passed. And they would sit upon some grassy, daisy-sprinkled mound, and he would tell her legends of old Rome, drawn from rare manuscripts in monkish piles or the worm-eaten pages of some forgotten historian, — legends perchance rejected by this learned age, but fresh and full of human interest, clothing dry Latin bones with lusty life, filling Time's empty vase with generous wine, casting the glory of heroic deeds over the wasted, silent battle-field, stretching so bare, so death-like still before them.

Then, when they reached their home, seated beside him on the stone balcony above the garden, overlooking the long reach of the Campagna, she would spend hours in dreamy revery, half unconsciously watching the long rows of broken aqueducts, the outlines of the distant hills, the gray walls of the far-off towns nestling in their rocky fastnesses, till the changing tints of molten gold, of Tyrian purple, and of deepest blue, which enveloped the distance as the sun went down, would warn them to withdraw, and seek the shelter of the ancient saloon within.

It was a lofty and deep embrasured room, canopied with gloom, curtained with shadow, its darkness but half illuminated by its lamps and candelabras of curious workmanship and ancient form. Old family portraits looked down from the walls, — pictures of defiant soldiers, crafty statesmen, majestic prelates, lofty dames, and inscrutable maidens. The furniture of tarnished magnificence, — red velvet chairs with carved ebony frames, old cabinets of labyrinthine compartments, inlaid with ivory, sculptured with armorial bearings;

tables of pictured mosaic, cracked and unsteady;
tabourets of faded tapestry, embroidered by dainty
fingers, whose very bones were now dust, — was
redolent of the past. All spoke of decayed splendor, of vanished riches; of haughty, humbled
pride.

In the gloomy entrance to the excavations of
Domitian's villa, beneath the velvet, air-spread
carpet of the Barberini pines, grow graceful wild
flowers, with curved white petals, crimson tipped.
They smile softly from the sullen shadow around
them; they cheer the eye with their sweet, languid grace. So Lilian bloomed and smiled amid
the shade of that old Italian mansion, shedding
the perfume of her life and love through its darkened chambers, filling the air with beauty and
delight.

———

LII.

It was high festival in Rome. Forth from the
narrow, dark, and winding streets, from their
dwellings by the turbid river-side, from their holds
on the narrow island, from their lurking-places in
ruined palaces, from their abodes beneath the
crumbling walls of ancient Rome, from their huts

on the Campagna, from their distant towns and hamlets amid the hills, towards St. Peter's poured the multitude, gorgeous in holiday array. Groups of proud maidens from the Trastevere, — their antique profiles showing, like the paintings on some old Etruscan vase, their raven hair coiled in classic mode low on their massive necks, and fastened by a glittering silver poniard, — slowly advanced, scarcely deigning to cast a glance upon the bronzed contadine in their crimson bodices, their snowy folded head-dresses, and laced kerchiefs, who pressed beside them towards the wide piazza of the great Cathedral. Bands of shepherds and goatherds, — their tall, conical caps garnished with peacock's feathers, shaggy mantles of goat-skin hanging from their shoulders, their thighs encased in breeches of dark blue, their legs bound with yellow buskins, — mingled, laughing and jesting, with the ever-increasing crowd, through whose midst rolled an endless stream of carriages towards the holy place. Golden-haired English-women, sparkling French, blue-eyed Russians, graceful Poles, flashing Spaniards, stately Austrians, delicate Americans, — all were there; all, according to time-hallowed custom, robed and veiled in black.

Up the long, sloping ascent, across the broad,
flag-paved steps, under the colossal portico, between the giant gates of sculptured bronze, into
the gorgeous temple, thronged the multitude: gray-
headed age and wondering childhood, smiling
youth and sturdy manhood, dark-eyed maidens
and brown-cowled friars, portly matrons and
swaggering soldiers, high-bred ladies and crippled
beggars, epauletted officers and veiled nuns; all
ranks, all ages, all degrees, pouring together, in
wide-spreading waves of human life, up the far-
lessening perspective of the polished pavement,
towards the endlessly-retreating sunlight of the
pictured, pillared dome.

A misty softness tempered the brightness of the
costly marbles, the splendor of the gilded capitals.
A gentle haze veiled the distant glories of the ceiling; a dim vapor, as of a thousand censers, hung
over the countless lamps and chiselled images, sub-
duing all things to religious awe. The air came
warm as from Judean plains, wafting a heavy
fragrance of frankincense and myrrh. A subtle
languor crept through Lilian's frame, tears rose
unbidden to her eyes, the sentiment of unquestion-
ing reverence stole over her, enchaining sense and
soul.

" And this cost the Reformation," said Mr. Clinton, who, with penetrating eye, had watched her changing, expressive face.

As if a trumpet had sounded in her ear, Lilian started. The enchantment weaving around her vanished like a sorcerer's spell before the holy sign. Her eye sank through the shining floor into underground, slowly dropping dungeons, filled with white, wan wretches, waiting the cruel wheels, the murderous pulleys, the flaming piles, and open graves, which were alone to set them free. For the breath of sacred spices, a smoke as of fresh-spilled blood rose, spreading pall-like over the in-crusted magnificence around. It curled in heavy wreaths towards the uplifted cross, shrouding it from her sight; and from the covering mantle came a voice, low, distinct, and awful, — " Where is thy brother ? What hast thou done ? "

----♦----

LIII.

LILIAN was ushered to her seat in one of the reserved galleries which, from between twisted columns of alabaster, look down upon the ever-burning lamps around St. Peter's shrine. She took her place beside a young and graceful woman, richly clad in black velvet, fastened at her throat with a clasp of diamonds, a veil of costly lace draping her from head to foot. As the stranger turned her head, a flash of joyful surprise broke from her eyes. She impulsively raised Lilian's hand to her lips.

" Ah, Madame, have I the happiness to see you again ? " she exclaimed.

It was the danseuse, but changed·beyond recognition. The clustering curls which had formerly framed her face were drawn back in massive waving folds, entirely altering the whole character of her countenance, with her grave and rich dress changing her former romantic prettiness into an air of gentle, quiet dignity.

" I am glad that you spoke to me, otherwise I should not have known you," said Lilian.

" I am rejoiced that you say so, Madame," answered her companion. I should be sorry to be recognized, for his sake." And there was a sorrowful intonation in her voice. " But that is my idea, Madame," she added quickly. " He is too kind ever to say so. He is so very kind ! " And her eyes beamed as she spoke.

" I see that I need not ask if you are happy," said Lilian.

"Ah, yes, Madame, I am very happy! He has pensioned my father, on condition that he never sees me again; and I am as happy as the day is long, except when I think of my poor mother. And there is one other thing. I am so very ignorant, Madame!" And she blushed deeply. "I did not know, when I was married, that I was to be *une grande dame*, else I should not have dared. But after I was married, I found that my husband was very rich; and, oh, how I cried! I wanted to leave him and go to school, but he said I was foolish, and would not hear of it. He said that he liked me very well as I was, but that if I wanted to learn, I might study at home. So I have an English *dame de compagnie*, and a great many masters, and I study very hard. But look! *le Saint Père!*" And she fell on her knees, devoutly crossing herself, as up the far distance of the nave, between the kneeling ranks of the vast multitude, in solemn procession, came the white-robed Pope, escorted by the crimson-mantled cardinals.

The censers smoked, the music pealed, the silver trumpets rang, the stately ritual drew on to its close. The pageant was over; they rose to descend. They passed down the staircase, and stood at the open door.

"Adieu, Madame," said the Frenchwoman, as their husbands advanced to rejoin them. "We leave Rome to-morrow. I may never see you again. May all happiness attend you, no evil ever befall you. Farewell."

———◆———

LIV.

Through the dim twilight of the great saloon, Lilian and Mr. Clinton paced up and down. As they reached the farthest end of the room, Lilian's eyes ever turned, as if fascinated, to a picture in a tarnished frame, on which the full, upward light of a lamp was cast. It was the portrait of a young woman, in the dress of long past times. Her hair of greenish gold, drawn back from her forehead, fell in serpentine masses upon her dead, white shoulders. The flesh tints of her face had sunk into the canvas, leaving it of a ghostly pallor, from which her emerald eyes gleamed with a sinister light. Her lips, red as a vampire's, were parted with a wily, watchful smile. Her right hand, resting on her opal jewelled stomacher, held a bunch of purple flowers, whose dark tints stood out in sharp relief against the faded sea-green brocade of her dress.

By an accidental effect, the light from below fell on the eyes of the picture in such manner that they seemed, as Lilian passed, to cast a furtive glance, quickly withdrawn, upon a portrait in the shade of the side wall. It was the likeness of a young girl of great beauty, clad in white satin. The heavy, shining folds were looped up from her soft arms, and gently rounded bosom, by pendant pearls, mingled with rubies, hanging like blood-drops. Her brown eyes were cast smilingly down upon a tiny spaniel, which was crouching upon a table by her side, apparently restrained from springing forward, by the pressure of her delicate hand. On her finger glittered the betrothal ring. On the table beside her was a princely coronet.

As she stood half turned, she appeared to be withholding the spaniel from attacking, with futile rage, the lady with the emerald gleaming eyes.

Lilian paused before the last portrait.

" It is strange that I should find my eye so constantly drawn to this picture, for I always look unwillingly. It invariably gives me a disagreeable sensation. I wish I knew her story. It would set my imagination at rest."

" It is a face belonging to a character, the product of a most vicious age," answered Mr. Clin-

ton. " We never see such faces now. They have
passed away with the peculiar circumstances which
developed the traits that stamp them. An edu-
cated criminal is an anomaly in our century.
Crime and degradation are now and will be hence-
forth as closely associated as crime and power were
then. Not but that noble characters were to be
found in the highest, and consequently the most
depraved, circles of those times. Here, for example, is a face which, young as it is, bespeaks
rare depth of feeling and constancy of purpose."
He led her before the portrait of a young girl of
perhaps fifteen.

According to a not unfrequent caprice of taste
in former days, she was portrayed with the attri-
butes of Saint Catherine; by her side a dark,
shining wheel, in her hand the martyr's branch
of palm. Heavy, low-toned draperies veiled the
girlish figure, — slender and stately as a cypress-
tree, — and mingled with the cloudy shadows of
the background. All the light of the picture was
concentrated on the face. The deep, inscrutable
eyes, the steady brow, the even nostril, the closely-
guarded mouth, the strongly accented chin and
cheek, — all were full of wakeful repose, of cautious penetration, of immutable will.

" Here also is forcibly marked the effect of an education foreign to our feelings, impossible to the social constitution of our day. As you look, you see that this girl is treading perforce a difficult, dangerous path. Resolution, prudence, foresight, are already fully developed in this young face.

" Yes, she must have been a noble creature," replied Lilian. " Her face is like the antidote to that baneful apparition opposite. She interests me quite as much, though in a different way. But is there no possibility of finding out their histories? Surely there must be old family records."

" Il Signor Dottore Albertazzi."

Mr. Clinton's lips were closely pressed together, as the ponderous curtain of the door was drawn aside, to give entrance to a small, dark, strongly-built man, with a thoughtful, compact head, flashing, restless eyes, strongly indicated nose and chin, and firm but kindly mouth.

The visitor hastened to meet his advancing host, and cordially grasped his outstretched hand.

" I have just returned to Rome, and I hasten at once to see you, my dear Mr. Clinton. I rejoice to meet you again under such happy auspices." And he turned, with a courteous salutation, towards Lilian.

“ Lilian, Dr. Albertazzi, a valued friend of mine,” said Mr. Clinton, with a slight air of constraint.

“ And the blow, — it had no awkward after-consequences ? ” inquired the physician, looking scrutinizingly at the massive locks which hung around Mr. Clinton’s temples.

“ None,” he answered, with evident effort.

The visitor pursued the subject no further. What blow ? Who was this stranger, a valued friend of whom Mr. Clinton had never spoken to her ? Why did he change countenance when this guest was announced, and why. did he look so pale and grave ? Lilian sat perplexed and disquieted, her eyes fixed upon her husband, whose face was gradually reassuming its wonted calmness.

“ You find us quite on the outskirts of the city ; but I was assured that the air is good, and we like the retirement.”

“ And the garden is delightful,” added Lilian, forcing herself to join in the conversation.

“ Yes, the garden I remember well. It is one of the pleasantest in Rome,” replied the Italian, bending his·head towards her, as if to catch every accent of her sweet, low voice. “ It is sunny, and full of birds and flowers, just the place for a lady young and like yourself.”

The tone was so frank and cordial that Lilian forgave the implied compliment, and smiled as she answered, —

" But I like other things, besides sunshine and birds and flowers. This old shadowy room that refuses obstinately to allow itself to be made cheerful, these antiquated chairs and sofas, these curious cabinets, and, most of all, these family portraits, delight me. I think that we of America must value such things more than any other people, for you know that we have nothing old. When I was a child, I used often to walk half a mile to see an old broken shed; and I looked at it with veneration, because I had been told it was a ruin. We have no ruins."

" And we have little else," replied the Italian, sadly. " St. Peter's great dome itself, like the religion preached beneath it, is falling to decay, each held in its place only by an iron chain."

He stopped, and a deep contraction furrowed his olive forehead.

" Mrs. Clinton was wishing, just as you came in, that she could learn something of the intimate history of the originals of these portraits," said Mr. Clinton, coming to Lilian's aid to turn the conversation. " Doubtless there are annals of the family."

“ Beyond a doubt such annals exist in the library of the palace in the Corso, but I fear they are as inaccessible as the archives of the Vatican, and for much the same reason.”

“ What, was this family so very wicked ? ” said Lilian, with a glance at the dimly-seen faces in the background.

“ It was wicked, like all the other great families. I do not mean to imply that the Ormanoni had instituted any monopoly of crime,” replied the Italian ; “ but if you are curious to hear old histories of the race, you should apply to *la vecchia* downstairs, Anina, the porter’s mother. She knows them all, and would be infinitely gratified at being called upon to instruct you. It still happens occasionally, that you find here servants, whose ancestors for many generations have been attached to the same family. They preserve unbroken the traditions of the house they serve, and their accounts are often more trustworthy than those of the paid and bribed annalist. Yes, I counsel you to send for old Anina.”

“ I shall certainly send for her to-morrow morning, according to your recommendation,” said Lilian. “ I shall have her brought into this room, and shall look at the pictures all the while she is telling me their stories. I am sure there is some tragedy connected with the life of that woman in sea-green brocade."

The Italian rose and approached the picture.

"Ah, yes, she poisoned her cousin!" Lilian looked aghast. "I have forgotten the story," he continued. "I only remember the fact. But old Anina will know."

"I see that the villa beside us is occupied within the last day or two," said Mr. Clinton, ever anxious to have only happy subjects brought before Lilian's excitable imagination. "You must know that we lead such secluded lives, that we are aware of little that passes around us, and are ignorant even of the names of our neighbors; so I apply to you to inform us who the remarkably pretty young girl is who has taken up her abode so near us."

"She is the young Marchesa Contini," answered the Italian. "Hers is a love-story. All Rome is talking about it. She was married three days ago, on the day she was to have taken the veil. The Marchese, her husband, had been betrothed as soon as he was born, to his cousin. But, as usually happens in such cases, when he grew up he fell in love with somebody else. The cousin on her side, — one of the most amiable young women in the world, — was equally averse to the union, for she had a vocation and was bent upon taking the veil. But the family took no heed of their unwillingness, and it was formally announced that they were to be married. The Contessina Carlotta could have been managed, for she was of a yielding disposition, but the young Marchese was rebelliously firm. He declared in reply to the formal announcement, that he would marry no one but the girl he loved, — the daughter of an old Cavaliere without a *bajocchio.* So his family set to work, and by means of the ghostly influence of which his uncle the Cardinal disposed, the old Cavaliere was persuaded that it was his duty to put his daughter into a convent, of which it was promised him she should eventually become abbess. She was entered as a novice, before the young Marchese knew anything about it. He was half distracted, and they sent him off to travel, — the invariable prescription, you know.

" The year was almost ended, when providentially the old Marchese died. The young man hurried back to Rome, immediately on receiving the intelligence. He arrived only a few days before she was to take the final vows. As soon as he reached his home, he convoked his whole family, uncles and aunts and cousins, and before them all took a solemn vow never to marry any one, — in which case one of the most ancient houses in Rome, with all its honors and dignities, would become extinct, — unless he married the novice. He added a second vow, never to ask absolution from the first, and then walked out of the room. You can imagine the dismay of the assembled conclave. All had had something to do with the affair, and all abused each other. At length they agreed on one thing: that the novice must be taken out of the convent and given to the Marchese, and so she was. As I said, they were married three days ago, on the day that had been appointed for her taking the black veil. He brought her to the Villa Contini, and there they are passing their first happy days."

The conversation rolled on in an even channel. No allusion was made, no reference occurred by which Lilian could guess at the association which had so overshadowed her husband's brow at the first entrance of their visitor.

As the curtain fell and the door closed behind

the parting guest, Mr. Clinton threw himself on a sofa and shaded his face with his hand. Lilian placed herself by his side, saddened and pondering. Could it be anything that had to do with his great sorrow? She slid her hand into that beside her. He looked up and met her gaze.

"He was on board The Ercolano when she ran us down," he said.

Lilian's heart sickened with sympathetic pain. On one subject they never spoke together. The name of Mira was never mentioned by either. It was no sullen secret, no gloomy mystery that closed his lips, no retrospective jealousy that sealed her speech. It was simply that the sudden and dreadful death of his young wife had been to him the cause of such exquisite and enduring suffering, that both shrank from sending his thought back from the sweet gladness and soft pleasure of his daily life, down to those cold depths wherein eternal darkness and silence, amid creeping sea-monsters and shapeless forms of dread, ungathered, uncoffined, still locked in the convulsion of her death-struggle, Mira's bones lay beneath the sea.

Lilian rose and knelt beside him on the sofa. She silently entwined her arms about his neck, and pressed close, clinging kisses on his forehead. He wound his arms around her and drew her to his knee. He buried his face in her bosom, as if seeking refuge from the anguish of past grief.

Gradually the soft presence of the woman he loved soothed his thought. He raised his head, rose, and drew her to the window.

" Let us go out on the balcony," he said.

The room seemed full of pain. Lilian was glad to escape from it to the moonlight without. It was a magical scene. The moon shone high in the heavens, effulgent amid the lesser stars, pouring floods of golden light over the gardens below. The vast expanse of the Campagna beyond lay veiled in silver mist, and in the distance, dream-like visions of far-off hills and mountains lifted themselves softly against the deep purple of the sky. The air, warm with the breath of spring, brought the rich odors of flowers and scented shrubs to their sense ; and, mingling with the faint tinkling of the waters of the fountains, rose the soft notes of a solitary nightingale, singing in the shade. They breathed in Beauty, they inhaled Peace. The shadow of their trouble passed away, and the still thankfulness which made the daily sunlight of their hearts, returned.

As they stood gazing with eyes' that wearied not, on the fair-spread scene beneath them, forth from the open windows of the neighboring villa floated a manly voice singing in careless cadence of improvisation:

Soft is the perfumed air,
  Sweet is the bird's low song,
Tenderly lie the clouds
  The midnight sky along.
Gently the moon's mild beams
  Rest on yon far-off height,
Whilst the Campagna's sea
  Sleeps, veiled in silver light.

Soft are thy kisses, love,
  Sweet is thy murmured tone;
Tenderly lies thy head
  My throbbing heart upon.
Gently, ah dear one, rest,
  Rocked by my happy sighs,
Until to-morrow's light
  Beams from the sunny skies.

The melody died away, and again they heard only the distant tinkling of the fountains and the low chant of the hidden bird.

"The air seems softer, the odors sweeter for the song," said Lilian. "How pleasant it is to think of the happiness so near us! What a change for that girl, — a week ago in a little bare cell in a walled convent, thinking herself divided forever from her lover, and now in the freedom of this lovely country-seat, with him."

"You think of her, as is natural," replied Mr. Clinton. "I think of him. Imagine what he must have felt when the woman he loved was separated from him, her life wearing away in her desolate convent, her heart wasting in the vain attempt to stifle out her love, or breaking in unresisting despair. I cannot bear to think of it," he said with sudden passion.

Lilian looked up in his face with the smile of perfect security, but as she saw its emotion, she remembered that such misery or worse, had already been his. Her eyes filled with tears and sank, — sank low and lower till they rested on the white sarcophagus. The same vague terror that she had felt at its first sight, returned upon her.

"Harvey, I am afraid of that sarcophagus," broke almost involuntarily from her lips.

Half reproachfully he answered her tone of distress.

"Why did you not tell me? If I could have fancied that it would have suggested any painful thought, I would have had it removed before I brought you here. It shall be taken away tomorrow. But why did you not tell me?"

"I was ashamed, it seemed so foolish. But why is it that the sight of it frightens me?"

"Probably because you know that it is a marble coffin. Its beauty does not alter, it only adorns its use. You may not have said this to yourself, but you must have unconsciously felt it and been disquieted by the obtruding of the sad associations of mortality into what I had hoped would be to you a garden of pleasure. But it shall be taken away to-morrow."

"Oh no, pray do not have it removed," pleaded Lilian. "I should be ashamed of my unreasonableness every time that I saw its empty place. And what have I to dread!"

As she ceased, through the night and stillness mournfully sinking, came the sound of a convent bell.

—◆—

LV.

"Eccomi quà, Signora mia, per servirla," said old Anina, as on the next morning she hobbled into the great, old-fashioned room, whose shadows, chased by the sunlight which streamed in through the open windows, had retreated to the heavily-carved cornices and ceiling, whence they gloomed sullenly down on the speakers below,—

old Anina, her gray hair tightly braided on her wrinkled brown forehead, and drawn back under a black silk coif; long golden pendants of rude workmanship dangling from her ears and resting on her shoulders, a string of golden beads encircling her withered neck, a scarlet kerchief folded over her bosom, a short brown stuff-petticoat showing her dark blue stockings and heavy shoes. Lilian, in her flowing robe of softest, whitest wool, fastened at her throat and waist by heavily tasselled crimson cords, her dark hair confined by a crimson net; the wrinkled, quick-eyed, alert age of the servant opposed in strong, yet harmonious contrast to the soft grace, the sweet youth of the lady.

" Sit here, Anina," said Lilian, pointing to a chair in the sunlight. " I have sent for you because I want to hear the stories of some of these portraits, and Dr. Albertazzi tells me that you know them all."

" Ah, what a good man is that Signore dottore ! What a sweet gentleman ! Yes, my beautiful lady, I know them all. I will not shame the Signor dottore, that good gentleman; I will tell them to you, all. Just as many as there are, so many will I tell you."

“ First I want to know the names and stories of these three portraits,” said Lilian, somewhat alarmed at the prospect of interminable narration opening before her. “ What was the name of this lady in sea-green brocade, and of this young girl in white satin, and of this one, younger still, with a branch of palm in her hand ? ”

“ The lady in the beautiful sea-green dress was Donna Apollonia, but she was not an Ormanoni at all. She has no right to be hanging up there, but so the old Signore would have it in his day, and of course it has never been touched since.”

“ And the young girls ? ”

“ She in the white satin with the great rubies and pearls, was Donna Flavia, and she with the palm branch, Donna Vittoria. They were sisters. Donna Apollonia was their cousin.”

“ Was it one of these that she poisoned ? ”

“ Ah, la Signora already knows something ! Yes, it was one of·these. But it is a long story. It has a beginning, and I must begin at the beginning.”

“ Wait till I have placed myself where I can see all three of the faces at once,” said Lilian, and she rolled an old couch opposite the angle where the three portraits were hanging. “ Now Anina, begin.”

" You must know, my beautiful lady, that the Duke Lorenzo, the father of Donna Flavia and Donna Vittoria, had been betrothed to the eldest daughter of the Marquis Menzone. It was an arrangement made as was usual in those days, before the children were born. The first child of the Marquis was a boy, so the little Duke Lorenzo had to wait still longer for his *promessa sposa*, and when she came at last, there were two of them, and in the confusion and the fright, — for the Marchesa, poor lady, was very ill, so that she died, — no one could remember which child was born first, and was consequently to marry Don Lorenzo. They did not know what to do. The only thing certain was that he was to marry one of them. At length the fathers agreed that when the time came, Don Lorenzo should choose the one he liked best, which was an unheard-of thing, and proves how much indulged Don Lorenzo must have been. So they grew up all three together, but every one knew from the time they were little things which of the sisters would be the Duchess. Donna Lucrezia was tall and fair, she had golden hair and a skin like milk. But she was cruel even as a little child. She used to set traps for the little

birds in the garden, and used to take the gold-
fishes out of the basins and laugh as they sprang
about on the grass. Donna Emilia used to cry
and put them back as soon as Donna Lucrezia's
back was turned, and she used to bury tenderly
the little dead birds, but she never dared oppose
her sister in anything to her face, because Donna
Lucrezia was so overbearing. Donna Emilia was
not so beautiful as her sister, she was as dark as
Donna Lucrezia was fair, but all the beauty that
she lacked in her outward form she possessed in
her soul. She was as gentle and mild as an angel. All the *servitu* adored her, but they could
not abide Donna Lucrezia. Don Lorenzo loved
her with all his heart, and when she was unhappy
because of her sister's unkindness, he would comfort her and tell her not to cry, for that she should
be his little wife. And he never varied in his
choice, although when the sisters grew up and
began to look womanly, Donna Lucrezia seemed
to lay aside her evil ways, and smiled softly and
moved gently and appeared quite changed. But
any one could see to look in her eyes that the
wickedness was still in her heart. She did all
that she could to lure Don Lorenzo away from
her sister, but it was all in vain. They were

married with great pomp on the day that Donna Emilia was sixteen. People at the wedding saw how ghastly pale Donna Lucrezia looked, and how full of wicked light her eyes were at the wedding-feast, but no one could see what lay coiled at her heart.

" A little while afterward Donna Lucrezia was married to a rich Florentine noble, and went to Florence to live. Her husband was rich, but not so rich as Don Lorenzo, and instead of being handsome and young, he was ugly and old, and had already had two wives. In a year after she was married, she had a daughter, Donna Apollonia. She never had any other children. The year afterward her husband died suddenly, leaving her all the estates he could dispose of. The rest went of course to Donna Apollonia.

" Years went by, four years, and Don Lorenzo and Donna Emilia had no children. It was their only grief. They tried all sorts of penances and pilgrimages to obtain the gift of a child, and at length to the great delight of the whole house, Donna Flavia was born. To be sure it was only a daughter, but they had waited so long that it was as much to them as a son would have been to any one else. Two years afterwards Donna Vittoria was born. This time they were sadly disappointed, and when the midwife showed the child to Donna Emilia, she burst into tears. But the midwife, who was learned in the stars, told her not to grieve, for that the child was born in the conjunction of Mercury and Jupiter, and would excel all the females of the house in wisdom and strength. So Donna Emilia dried her tears and welcomed the child gladly.

" The prediction of the midwife was verified from the beginning. She was the most patient of little children even before she could speak, and she was as just as the Good Lord himself, while she was still creeping on the floor. Her nurse, as was to be expected, loved her better than she did Donna Flavia, and one day as she was giving them strawberries in the garden, she gave Donna Vittoria two in succession, instead of giving the second to Donna Flavia as she ought to have done. Donna Flavia began to cry, for she was always soft-hearted, but Donna Vittoria would not eat the strawberry, she squeezed it into Donna Flavia's hand, and the juice ran down and spoiled her satin dress, and then she slipped out of her nurse's arms and toddled up to Donna Flavia and hugged her and

kissed her, and she would not eat any more
strawberries she was so angered with her nurse.
— The nurse was an ancestress of mine. — It was
a little thing, but all her life when a child was
made up of things like that.

"Any one would have thought to have seen them
together that Donna Vittoria was the oldest. She
soon grew taller than her sister, though she was
always slender, and she watched over her and
took care of her, from the time they were little
creatures. She was gentle and kind to all, ever
respectful and obedient to her parents and instruc-
tors, but she never seemed really to love any one
save Donna Flavia, and she would have given her
life to please her. And Donna Flavia loved her
just as well, only in a different manner, according to the difference between them. She obeyed
every word Donna Vittoria said, and leaned upon
her in all things. It was beautiful to see them
together.

"When Donna Flavia was seventeen, she was
universally accounted the loveliest young lady in
Rome. You see her in her portrait as she was.
She was not betrothed, and she had many suitors,
but the one her parents chose was the Principe di
Terracina, the greatest match in Rome. He was

very young and desperately in love. And all the family were very glad because of this great match.

" Just a little while after they were promised to each other, the sister of Donna Emilia, Donna Lucrezia, died, and left her only child, Donna Apollonia, to Don Lorenzo and Donna Emilia's care. So they sent for her to Florence and had her brought to Rome. Donna Emilia, who had not seen her sister since her marriage, and who had grieved very much at her death, for she was of a forgiving disposition and had forgotten all about her unkindness years before, was quite overcome at the sight of her niece, who was the very image of her mother, and took her at once to her heart. Donna Apollonia had the most gracious, winning ways in the world: her voice was as sweet as a purple fig, her motion as gliding as a lizard's, and she always dressed in green. She seemed to bewitch the whole house and everything in it, except Donna Vittoria and Donna Flavia's pet spaniel. He had always before been a good-natured and polite dog, but whenever he saw Donna Apollonia, he barked himself hoarse, would run at her as if to bite her, then put his tail between his legs, yelp, and run back to

Donna Flavia, who was much scandalized at his want of good-breeding.

" Donna Apollonia, from the time of her entrance into the house, attached herself particularly to Donna Flavia. She sang to her the new romances that she had brought with her from Florence; she taught her to play upon a newly-invented lute; she arranged flowers in her hair in the most becoming manner; and she used to talk to the Principe, when he made his visits; — for which last thing Donna Flavia was especially grateful, for she was very shy, and blushed up to the eyes whenever he spoke to her.

She never tried to ingratiate herself with Donna Vittoria, after the first few days, but, on the contrary, seemed to avoid all occasions of being left alone with her. Donna Vittoria once tried to put Donna Flavia on her guard against her cousin, but for the first time she found her words unheeded. Donna Flavia kissed her, and told her that if she only knew how Donna Apollonia admired and praised her behind her back, she would never think unkindly of her again. Donna Vittoria shook her head, and went away, for she saw that she was not strong enough to struggle with the artfulness of a woman so much older than she was.

" The time for Donna Flavia's marriage approached; but first, of course, her picture was to be painted; and the Duke and Duchess said that they would have Donna Vittoria's and Donna Apollonia's painted at the same time. A great painter was sent for, and a room fitted up as a studio. They were allowed to choose their own dresses, and Donna Flavia and Donna Apollonia chose those you see; but when they asked Donna Vittoria what she would have, she said the artist could choose for her better than she could for herself, so he painted her as Santa Caterina.

" When the artist was about to begin, Donna Flavia wanted to have her little dog painted too on the table beside her. He said it would do very well, so the little dog was put there, and sat very quiet and contented till the door opened, and Donna Apollonia glided in. As soon as he saw her, the little dog crouched down as if to spring at her, and snarled and showed his teeth. Donna Flavia put her hand on him to hold him still, and scolded him, smiling the while to see him in such a rage. The artist said that she must be painted just so, and he painted her just as she stood at that moment, only the Principe insisted upon having the coronet she was to wear as his wife, put in. — Poor Donna Flavia!

"The great artist seemed very happy while painting Donna Flavia and Donna Vittoria, but when he came to paint Donna Apollonia's portrait, he grew very strange. His eyes would contract as he looked at her, and he would gnaw his lip as he laid the colors on the canvas. He grew pale and thin, and got a strange nervous look as the picture went on. At length her portrait also was finished, except some touches on the drapery in the corner. She came approaching with her noiseless step to look at it. He was busy painting, and did not know she was by him, until he looked up and saw her at his side. He sprang up straight, shouted out at her, 'Avaunt thee, Satan!' threw down his brush, and rushed out of the palazzo. Donna Apollonia turned green, but said not a word. Donna Flavia threw her arms round her neck, kissing her and caressing her, and Donna Vittoria walked out of the room. The artist would never come back; and, if you look close, you will see that the picture is unfinished in the corner to this very day."

It was true. As Lilian fixed her eyes upon the draperies, there was an obvious want of finish in the lower folds.

"The week before the wedding came, the

palace was in a great ferment with the preparations for the wedding and the wedding-feast.
Splendid presents were sent to Donna Flavia, for,
as every one knows, the Ormanoni are connected
with all the great families in Rome.   Donna
Apollonia sat all the time busily embroidering a
silken girdle that she was to wear at the wedding.
It was white, worked with purple flowers.   She
took no part in the bustle, but sat with her head
bent over her work all the time, day and night.
For that whole week every night, light shone
through the crack under her door; and, when
some one remarked on it, she answered that she
had work to do at night to be ready for the wedding.   One day, contrary to her custom, Donna
Vittoria came near her and looked at her work.
'Your flowers look poisonous, Apollonia,' she
said; and just at that moment, Donna Apollonia
gave a start, and ran the needle deep into her
hand. The blood dropped, but Donna Vittoria
did not stop to pity her, and went on her way.

"The week passed;—it was the eve of the wedding day.   Donna Flavia's wedding-dress of white
brocade, embroidered with great bunches of flowers
as large as life, was laid in her room, ready for
the morning.   Her parents kissed and blessed her,

and Donna Vittoria held her long and silently in her arms, before they parted for the night. 'Felicissima notte,' said Donna Apollonia; and her face was as white as a ghost's.

"That night all the household on that story slept as if they had fallen into an enchanted slumber. It was very late before any one awoke, and when they did wake, their eyes were heavy and their heads swam. They did not know what was the matter. They rose, and, as soon as they were ready, they hurried into Donna Flavia's room, to dress her for her marriage. She had not waked. They called her, but she did not answer. They threw back the shutters, and let the sunlight into the room, and there, in her bed she lay, dead, with a bunch of flowers which the Principe had gathered for her as they were walking in the garden the day before, resting on the pillow by her head.

"'Oh, the flowers, the wicked flowers, they have poisoned her to death!' shrieked Donna Apollonia, who was with the first who entered the room, and she caught them up, and rushed into the antechamber, where was a brazier of burning coals, and threw them in it. A suffocating smell immediately filled the antechamber, and Donna

Flavia's little bird, which hung there, fluttered its wings, gasped, and fell down dead.

" They sent for all the doctors in Rome, but no one could bring her to life again. The doctors said that, doubtless, there had been some poisonous blossom among the flowers that the Principe had gathered, and it was that which had killed her.

" Donna Apollonia wept and raved and tore her hair ; the Duke and Duchess were crazy with grief; the Principe rushed about like a madman ; but Donna Vittoria stood like a stone beside her sister, and neither wept nor spoke, except to give the necessary orders, for the father and mother were in such a state that no one thought of applying to them. She had her sister dressed in her bridal robe and veil, and when all was finished, by her order every one went out of the room and left her alone with Donna Flavia. She stood at the foot of the bed and made a vow never to sleep in a bed nor to taste meat or wine, until she had avenged her sister's death.

" She watched by Donna Flavia until they came and carried her body to the church ; then she went to her father and mother and asked leave to go into retreat in a convent to pray for her sister's soul. They could not refuse such a pious request, so she went, taking with her Donna Flavia's little dog. She stayed there until, before the year was out, Donna Apollonia married the Principe di Terracina, who was to have been the husband of Donna Flavia. He was younger than she was, and people wondered very much; but she had bewitched him as she had the Duke and Duchess and all the house, and he was like a slave to her.

" After Donna Apollonia was married, Donna Vittoria left the convent and came home. Her parents were very much afraid that she would make herself a nun, for they saw that she never tasted meat or wine, and the servants told that her bed was never slept in, and they were very anxious to marry her at once. But she told them that they must let her choose a husband for herself, and they were afraid to contradict her, lest she should make herself a nun, so they promised.

" Many nobles wanted to marry her, for she was handsome, though not as beautiful as Donna Flavia had been, and she was very learned, and she composed beautiful poems which she sang to the lute, and she was also very rich; but she waited long before she made her choice. At length she chose the Principe Barberini, who had only recently lost his wife. He was a nobleman of great soul and honor, and a nephew of the Pope's. He was a friend of her father's, and of course a great many years older than she was. But before she promised herself to him, she told him of her vow, how she was sure that Donna Apollonia had poisoned Donna Flavia, and how she had vowed never to sleep in a bed nor to taste meat or wine until she had avenged her sister's death. And the Principe took a mighty oath to aid her by every means in his power, to fulfil her vow. So they were married. Such a wedding had never been seen in Rome. All the noble lords and ladies of the whole city and country round filled the church, not one was absent save Donna Apollonia. She sent word that she was ill and could not come. She also sent a present, a silver casket with a jewelled key, but Donna Vittoria did not open the casket, when it was brought to her, and it disappeared and nobody ever saw it again.

" After the wedding, the Duke and Duchess, by Donna Vittoria's request, went to Naples to change the air, and at her desire, they left with her Donna Flavia's portrait.

" A short time afterwards, all Rome was talking of a fortune-teller, who had come, no one knew whence. She lived in a little dark street near the Porta Salaria, and her door was opened only at midnight, and then but for an hour. She would tell fortunes to noblewomen only. No man was allowed to cross her threshold, and any woman not noble was instantly detected and sent away. She was immensely old and hideously ugly, people said, and all those that went to her agreed that her eyes pierced them through and through, and that her voice had a tone of authority in it, before which the haughtiest of them quailed.

" Veiled from head to foot, one midnight Donna Apollonia stood at the low door in the little dark street and knocked. It was opened by invisible hands and she entered a dimly-lighted hall. A catafalque of black, surrounded by extinguished candles in massy silver candlesticks, stood in the midst of the room, which was hung with black; the ceiling and the floor were also covered with black.

" Donna Apollonia had a hard, bold heart, but she was disquieted at the ghastly aspect of all around. She would have turned back, but the door whereby she had entered was invisible. As

she stood, the black hangings at the end of the
room slowly opened, and she heard a voice say,
' Approach.'   Before her, in another dimly-lighted, black-draped room, on a high, throne-like
seat, sat the sorceress.   She was an old woman
of wrinkled countenance ,and stooping figure.
Her eyes fixed upon Donna Apollonia with a
look that sent the blood to her wicked heart.
' Approach, unveil,' said the fortune-teller, and
Donna Apollonia advanced and threw back her
veil.   The old woman looked at her some moments without speaking, then, ' What do you
wish from me ? ' she said.   ' Good mother, I
would know what the stars have in store for
me,' replied Donna Apollonia, trying to steady
her voice.   ' Hold out your hand.'   Donna Apollonia held out her hand and the old woman bent
over it.   She studied it for a while, then, — ' You
were born afar,' she said.   ' Your father died suddenly, when you were a child.   Your mother died
but a few years ago.   Then your line of life breaks
into a long journey.   Your journey ends and your
line of life lies fair and even.   But here,' she said,
sinking her voice, — ' here blood crosses the line ! '
Donna Apollonia's knees shook.   ' Whose blood,
— speak ! ' — she said in a deep, menacing tone.

Donna Apollonia was dumb. The sorceress stamped on the floor. A curtain at the end of the room shook. She stamped again. It opened, and, as through a black shadow, Donna Apollonia saw the apparition of Donna Flavia as she stood when the artist painted her. She fell on her knees and clasped her hands over her eyes. 'Speak,' repeated the sorceress in awful tones. 'It was my cousin Flavia,' said Donna Apollonia in a thick, hoarse voice.

" The sorceress clapped her hands together. Another curtain opened and from the recess behind, the familiars of the Holy Office advanced, and laid hold of Donna Apollonia. She gave a horrid, strangled cry, and turned to the sorceress. An enamelled mask lay on the floor, a towering figure with terrible eyes stood where the sorceress had been, and she saw her cousin, Donna Vittoria, before her.

" No one ever knew what had become of Donna Apollonia. Search was made for her everywheres, but no clue was ever found.

" Four weeks after that night, a mass for the dead was celebrated in the Barberini Chapel, and Donna Vittoria again slept in a bed, and tasted of meat and wine."

20 *

“ That’s the story, my beautiful lady,” said old Anina as she ended. “ Now shall I tell you another ? ”

“ Mille grazie, Anina, not to-day. I am going now to walk in the garden,” replied Lilian, anxious to escape from the tainted atmosphere of crime which seemed to exhale from the portrait of Donna Apollonia, her pallid face lighted by her emerald gleaming eyes, from the contemplation of Donna Flavia’s ill-fated loveliness, and Donna Vittoria’s deep, sad, penetrating gaze.

“ Another day, then, as soon as your beautiful ladyship pleases. For I know them all, yes, all ! As many as there are, so many I know,” said old Anina, and she took her leave.

“ Oh, don’t go in there. Come down into the garden with me,” exclaimed Lilian, seizing Mr. Clinton’s hand as she met him in the antechamber.

“ What, has old Anina been frightening you with her stories ? ” he responded, looking down on her face.

“ No, not exactly, but it makes me feel uncomfortable to be in the room with the picture of that woman in green brocade. I want to get into the sunlight, and see the flowers, and think of something else," said Lilian, as they descended the broad staircase. And she passed the marble sarcophagus without her usual quiver, so filled was her mind with old Anina's story.

Through the pleasant paths winding among the little flower-sprinkled lawns they passed, silently enjoying the light, the warmth, the beauty around them. The heavy softness of the day filled Lilian's frame with languid delight. Not a cloud was in the sky, not a shadow on the landscape.

"Look at Giacomo," said Lilian as they turned into the long terrace walk. "See what a melancholy air he has, standing there with folded arms, looking at the laurel-tree behind the sarcophagus. What can be the matter with him?"

"Do you not see, — the tree is dying," replied Mr. Clinton; and as he spoke, as if his words had detached them from their stems, down floated a few yellow leaves through the sunny, stirless air.

"What is it, Giacomo?" said Lilian as they approached. "Why do you look so mournful?"

"Ah, Signora mia, I am sorry because of the tree. Its first leaf turned the day that the Signora and the Signore came here, and now see how yellow it is! I must cut it down, and that grieves me. The garden does not look natural to me again for a long time after it has lost a tree, and then, though it be only a tree, yet it is something that dies, and Death is always melancholy."

The faces of his hearers saddened and they walked on. As they passed before the sarcophagus, a new, motionless gust shook down the yellow leaves upon them.

LVI.

LILIAN, in her travelling-dress, walked slowly through the vast, shadowy rooms of the old Italian villa. Her heart was heavy, her face was sad. She stood and gazed, as if to imprint the aspect of each room indelibly upon her memory; the saloon, with its galleried portraits, its antique furnishing, the sunlight pouring in broad floods through the heavily-cased windows, thrown open to admit the morning air; the ample dining-room, with its dark, panelled walls and buffets of shining oak; her own room, its walls curiously adorned with mouldings of gilded arabesques, its frescoed ceiling, whence laughing children bent, throwing wreaths of flowers down on the sleepers below, its heavy commodes of variegated woods, mounted in gilded brass and supporting slabs of Asiatic marbles, its toilet-table with its small swinging mirror set in chiselled bronze, the lofty bed, its frame richly carved with stories of ancient Jewish loves; all these she looked upon as we look upon the face of a friend we love, and are to see no more.

She passed out upon the broad, stone balcony and gazed towards the distant hills. Never had they looked so sadly beautiful before. There seemed something reproachful in the sunny stillness of the Campagna. Her eyes wandered over the rich luxuriance of the garden below, so peaceful in its solitude. They fell upon the white sarcophagus. The tree that had stood behind it was gone. It stared up at her from the sunlight, blank, vacant, foreboding. A chill swept Lilian. She drew back. An angry spot flushed out upon her forehead. Her brows knit. Her lips closed firmly. " Was she then so weak! Had a marble stone power to terrify her ! "

She passed swiftly down the wide staircase, with its banded sunlight, through the dark entrance-hall, into the garden. She stood before the voiceless, threatening shell. She laid her hand upon it. She passed in slow, deliberate review each figure of the gleeful, dancing chain. Around it she glided, still she saw the same joyous troop, revelling in marble mockery of life. She passed to the farther side, shaded until that day by the woven branches of the laurel-tree. The dance had ceased. Aghast on either side, the dancers were fleeing from one figure in the centre, all save two, — a maiden and a man. They stood, their arms wound around each other, the maiden's face hidden on her lover's bosom in a vain attempt to find there safety from her approaching doom. By their side, the Genius of Death, with inverted torch, its veil thrown back, laid its hand upon the maiden's shoulder. The moment of separation had come. She must leave her lover. But was it for this that Lilian's breath failed, her head swam, and her knees sank under her? Was it that antique record of woe that reflected such answering terror on her face? No! From the reverted veil of the spectral visitant, its pure outlines sculptured line for line, looked out with regretful yet unyielding monition, the lifelike presentment of Mira. It was Mira who was tearing the maiden from that fond embrace, Mira who with unwavering hand was leading her from the gladness of her youthful love into the anguished night of separation. How many years had passed since Lilian had seen that face !— and there it stood, not chiselled in marble stone, but a presence, dimly foreboding, prophet of coming woe. As she gazed with sinking terror, it seemed to detach itself from the marble, to expand and fill the air. Lilian tottered and clung to the sarcophagus. A hasty step sprang through the hall.

" Lilian, Good God, what is it ! " exclaimed her husband as he caught her in his arms.

She hid her face in his bosom and pointed to the sarcophagus. He stood for an instant motionless, holding her fast. No word told her that he saw the apparition of his lost wife. Then she was lifted in his arms, carried through the hall, placed in the travelling-carriage, and she felt herself borne rapidly away.

She looked up at Mr. Clinton. His face was deathly pale. As he met her imploring gaze he folded her close to his heart, but spoke not.

She never knew if he had read like her that writing on the wall.

LVII.

To the glowing South, to the land of the myrtle. and the palm, the golden orange and the fragrant lime, the scarlet pomegranate and the luscious fig, the deep blue heaven and the deeper, bluer sea ; to a villa, through whose cool chambers the ceaseless murmur of the waves below made gentle music, over whose balconies jasmines and lemon-trees scattered their snowy blossoms before the gliding footsteps of the low whispering breeze, — thither Mr. Clinton bore Lilian, there they passed the long days and starlit nights of the Italian summer. And they were happy.

True, — as Mr. Clinton looked on the brightly-glittering waters, a half transparent figure would sometimes flit before him. As the wavelets broke on the smooth, shining sands, he would sometimes hear the far-off echo of a silent voice. But he would turn and look on Lilian's gentle face, — and the vision would vanish, and the far-off echo cease, and the unforgotten grief rest in its grave again.

And Lilian ? Every need of her heart, every aspiration of her nature was fulfilled.

No sudden, forced development of her affections had brought trouble into her soul. Her present was the perfect completion of her past. In harmonious succession, in increasing gradation, Mr. Clinton had aroused the profoundest emotions of her opening life, and each retained its sweetness and its power. The child's reverence deepened with holy trustfulness, the maiden's affection haloed with delicate reserve the impassioned love with which her whole being was transfused. Day followed night in golden circles of peace unshadowed, joy ineffable. The protecting care, the tender respect, the penetrating passion which filled the very air she breathed, seemed as a wall between her and the distant world without. If the remembrance of the dread that had smitten her, of the threatening omen that had flashed out upon her, still lived, it was as a little cloud, no bigger than a man's hand, resting low on the horizon of the sun-filled sky.

Their's was the perfection of human union, the fulfilment of God's sweetest, most glorious thought for man. And as fragrant incense, floated ever upward from their hearts, the still, ceaseless anthem, —

"Thanks, O great God! Thanks for life! Thanks for love! Thanks for each other!"

LVIII.

THERE was no moon, but the large, bright stars were reflected in silver lines upon the water, as Mr. Clinton and Lilian descended to the shore, where a fishing-boat, with its picturesque lateen sail, its flaming torches, and its bronzed, flashing-eyed crew awaited them.

"We shall have good luck to-night," said Bartolomeo, steadying the boat against the little jetty as Lilian took her place. "The fishes will all flock after us, to look at the beautiful face of the Signora. Our nets will be full."

The sail hung heavily against the mast, for the air was breathlessly still. The fishermen bent to their oars, and rowed out to the open sea. The torches shed broad, red bands of light upon the black water, and illumined the swarthy forms and faces before Lilian, as they rocked backwards and forwards, keeping time to their oars.

"Sing to us something," said Mr. Clinton; "it would please the Signora much."

"Anything to please the beautiful Signora," responded the spokesman of the party; and, after a few words interchanged with his companions, the rich Italian voices joined, raising a canzone,

free, bold, vigorous, each strophe ending in a prolonged minor modulation, inexpressibly mournful
in its effect.

There was something strangely pleasurable and
exciting in the sharp, strongly-accented contrasts
that reigned around. Lilian's face reflected each
change of the music; her eyes mirrored in succession the streaming, sparkling torches, and the
dark, mysterious sea.

The boat reached the distant fishing-ground.
The music gave place to the answering cries with
which the fishermen disentangled, shook out, and
sank the woven nets. Then, in profoundest silence, they watched and waited for their finny
prey.

The torches of the neighboring boats dotted the
water here and there; and against their light the
black outlines of the various crews stood out in
bold relief, touched with crimson reflections.

They had lain some time in silence, when Lilian laid her hand upon Mr. Clinton's.

" See that little cloud," she said.

A cloud no bigger than a man's hand rested
upon the horizon.

" Guardi, Bartolomeo! " said Mr. Clinton,
hastily, bending forward, and pointing to the
scarcely discernible vapor.

"Gesù!" he exclaimed. "Presto! presto! pull in the nets!—the tempest!"

Cries of hurry and alarm sounded over the water, as the boats around hurriedly drew up their nets and closely furled their sails.

Rapidly rose the cloud, darker and darker, more and more threatening. No breath ruffled the sea; it was still and smooth as a black mirror. The fishermen turned their faces anxiously upward. As the cloud reached the zenith, "Eccolo!" said Bartolomeo; and, with a mighty shrieking roar, the tempest burst upon them. In one instant, the sea was white as milk. The boat quivered as with fright, plunged as if to seek refuge under the waves, then, rising, fled amain before the fury of the blast.

Lilian leaned against Mr. Clinton's shoulder. She spoke no word, but, as his encircling arm rested beneath her heart, he could feel its rapid, heavy pulsations.

The storm-cloud spread until it covered the sky with its impenetrable mantle. The torches were extinguished. In total darkness, they drove before the wind. Through the vengeful howling of the tempest, Lilian could hear the terrified invocations of the fishermen, as they called upon their patron saints.

She could tell that the waves were rapidly rising, by the increased motion of the boat, and by the occasional dash of cold water upon her, as they broke over the low gunwale. Firmly Mr. Clinton held her to his side, and once in the darkness, amid the howling of the storm, she felt his lips pressed to her forehead.

Each moment threatened to whelm them in the cold abyss beneath; each moment the creaking, groaning boat tossed more wildly; each moment the waves broke higher over her dipping sides. Fast in the darkness, the fishermen baled against the ever-deepening water.

Lilian sat clinging around her husband's neck, strained close in his embrace. "Was their happy life to have this fearful ending!" Long past events in rapidly changing succession rose before her memory. Snatches of songs learnt in her childish days, burdens of airs long unheard, mingled with the quick dashing of the waves and the harsh shrieking of the blast.

At length, down, as though the heavens had fallen in one vast cataract, down dashed the torrents of the rain.

"Thanks be to the Holy Virgin, the Padre Eterno, and all the Saints!" she heard Bartolomeo's voice exclaim. And the fishermen baled with the redoubled energy of hope.

The mass of falling water seemed to beat down the furious waves. The boat plunged less deeply, the water poured less heavily over Lilian's dripping form. The wind was perceptibly sinking, though still the boat drove fast over the unseen expanse of the dashing, rolling sea. By degrees the rain ceased, the tempest raged itself into calm, and on the pale gray of the sky, they saw the faint red flush of dawn.

" Thank God ! " burst from Mr. Clinton's lips.

" Thank God ! " reëchoed from Lilian's voice. She lifted her eyes and saw through the pale light, her husband's face, the face she had thought never to see again.

" Capri," shouted Bartolomeo, as he pointed to a steep castle-like islet dimly rising from the tossing waves.

Mr. Clinton looked hurriedly around. A spasm passed over him. They were off the Bay of Naples !

Lilian felt with sympathetic anguish the sharptoothed memories that were fastening upon him, pouring up from the cold depths of the cruel sea. She clasped her hands together and bowed her head to conceal her fast-falling tears.

Mr. Clinton raised his gaze from the dark chasm where it had plunged. He turned it upon her.

"My wife," he said. She lifted her head, and as the bow of peace that half veiled in mist, hangs over Niagara's flood, so the look of love in her swimming eyes beamed on the swift-rushing torrent of his troubled thoughts.

"We must make for Capri, Signore," said Bartolomeo. "The boat leaks badly." And towards the precipitous rock the fishermen pulled in haste.

The waves broke heavily upon the brown walls of the rocky fortress, their shining green masses and sparkling white crests leaping aloft as if to scale its inaccessible height, then with an angry roar, rushing back again to renew their attack, again, hissing and foaming, to retreat. No landing seemed possible, until doubling the cliffs, they saw a green, sloping shore, peacefully extending, in the lee of which the waves were rocking quietly, as if unconscious of the battle raging without.

The fishermen threw themselves into the shallow water and dragged their shattered vessel towards the beach. Mr. Clinton, lifting Lilian in his arms, bore her to the shore.

High upon the grassy ascent stood a rude hut, built of discolored driftwood. Thither he carried her, chilled and exhausted, and knocked loudly at the door.

"Santissima Vergine, what has happened?" responded a high, cracked voice within.

"Strangers, — a lady," answered Mr. Clinton.

An old man in half-donned attire hastily opened the door, and with a shower of invocations and ejaculations, received his unexpected guests.

"Fire, can you make us a fire?" said Mr. Clinton as he bore Lilian into the shelter of the hut, and laying her down, spread over her the shaggy sheep-skins, the only coverings the dwelling afforded.

"Oh, yes, my blessed Signore. I will make in one very smallest instant a great fire to warm the lady's heart." And rushing out he returned speedily, bearing a load of broken driftwood, shattered planks and shivered spars.

"The sea provides for us, Signore, you see," said the old man, chuckling as he kindled the dry, quickly-blazing fragments. "Now I will run, prestissimo, up to Maddalena, my daughter, and bring her down to wait on the lady." And the old man departed in haste.

The cheerful blaze had already begun to warm Lilian's cold and stiffened limbs, when the door of the hut was opened, and a young woman of regular features, and low, sturdy form, entered. Her proud eyes softened, and her firm mouth relaxed, as she beheld the pallid countenance of the lady. She turned to Mr. Clinton.

" Signore, you must leave us. The signora must be put into dry, warm clothes." And unfastening a bundle that she had brought with her, she spread the gay articles of festal attire it contained around the sparkling fire.

" I will take care of her as if she were my own sister," said Maddalena, as Mr. Clinton with an anxious look at Lilian, withdrew.

The fire lighted up the hut with a ruddy glare, and flashed upon Maddalena's brown cheek, her red boddice, and black, plaited hair, as she drew forward a rude settle, and taking Lilian in her arms as if she had been a child, removed her wet clothing, chafed her cold hands and feet, and robed her in her own fresh bridal attire.

" Ah vedi, Signora, quanto sei bella ! " she exclaimed triumphantly as she completed Lilian's toilet, gazing with admiration at her, as she stood in the full-plaited sleeves and chemisette, the laced scarlet boddice, and the short, brilliantly striped skirt. "How much handsomer this dress is than that you had on!" and she glanced contemptuously at the garments of costly fabric which Lilian had quitted.

"Now, Maddalena, you may call the Signore. He will thank you as much as I do for all your kindness."

"No need of thanks," replied Maddalena. "What a heart of stone it would be that did not melt at the sight of such a face as yours!" And she looked with an air of protection and superiority upon the delicately-cut features of the American.

Lilian sat by her husband, beside the flickering, yellow flames of the fire,—too weary, too exhausted to think, yet enjoying, with quiet delight, the safety, the stillness, the warmth.

Gradually mingling with the sense of comfort, sleep stole over her. Her head drooped on her shoulder, her eyelids closed. She had a dim consciousness of being placed upon something rough and warm, then she knew nothing more till she was wakened by a heavy knock at the door, a rough voice outside, —

"All is ready, Signori, and the wind is fair."

Hastily she resumed her own dried garments, and, placing in the wondering hand of the old man a gold coin, to be given to Maddalena after their departure, she descended with Mr. Clinton to the shore, where the fishermen stood waiting by the rocking boat.

An indescribable dewy freshness filled the air. The morning sun in glad effulgence shone from the deep, transparent sky, while before him were fleeing trailing white clouds, the scattered rearguard of the tempest. The rejoicing sea danced and sparkled in the sunlight, and across its glittering expanse rose the gently curving shore, veiled in soft, ethereal blue. White birds rose, wheeled and chased each other in playful sport over the glancing waves, and little boats stretched their sails to the fresh breeze, and sped fast on their joyful way.

Again Lilian and her husband were in the rocking boat upon the sea. In darkness and dismay, they had driven before the tempest far from their home. In sunlight and gladness, they sought again its happy shelter. And the waves bore them on, — the waves, restless as human life, changeful as human weal, obedient in their restless changefulness to the One Inscrutable Will.

LIX.

LILIAN, clothed in black, stood by the open window of the palazzo. The discordant, mingling cries and gay laughter of the Neapolitan crowd came from the street beneath, unheard by her absent ear. She stood gazing between the flowering oleanders and the tall rose-trees of the balcony, her face turned towards the scene beyond. The waves, sparkling with diamond light, broke in soft ripples on the yellow sands. The sky above was one vast resplendent vault of blue, unflecked by even the smallest cloud, save where, behind her and out of sight, from the summit of Vesuvius, rose a dark, taper column of smoke. But Lilian's eyes saw not the beauty whereon they rested. Their sight was veiled with sorrowful memories.

A step approached her. Mr. Clinton took her hand in his, and stood silently beside her.

Lilian looked up wistfully.

"If I could only have seen her once more!" Her eyes filled with tears. She was pale. She had suffered.

"I am going to ask you to do what will cost you an effort," said Mr. Clinton. "The Thorntons, as you know, were to have sailed to-night in the Ischia, for Civita Vecchia, but they are detained. The son has got into trouble of some sort. I have just received a note from old Mr. Thornton, asking me to come there at once. It is the hour I appointed to go with the Vanes to Santa Lucia. The permission is given only to Mr. and Mrs. Clinton and party. They cannot go without one of us. Can you take my place? The carriage is at the door."

"If you wish it, certainly," replied Lilian; and in a few moments she stood before her husband, in her sombre drapery and sweeping black veil.

"There is the permission and the passport;" and he gave the papers into her hand. "I hope the air will bring a little color into your cheeks," he said, looking fondly on her sweet, sad countenance, as he led her down the staircase and placed her in the carriage. "We shall meet again in two hours." And he watched the carriage till it was out of sight.

LX.

" How you shudder, Mrs. Clinton," said young Harry Vane, as, leaning on his arm, Lilian crossed the threshold of the Hospital of Santa Lucia. " I shall believe that some one is walking over your grave."

Lilian forced a smile, and proceeded.

Mr. Clinton had not known how great was the demand that he was making upon his wife, when he asked of her to take his place. The terror of that last interview with Roger, those sinister words addressed to her so directly before his ghastly, self-inflicted death, had produced a permanent effect upon her imagination. The idea of any contact with madness was acutely painful to her.

As she passed the heavy portal of that sad palace of wandering Thought, an indescribable distress came over Lilian. A nameless fear seemed creeping before her, an invisible dread gliding behind her. Lurking shadows seemed peering in through the barred windows, dim apprehensions hiding in the dark niches.

They passed through spacious halls and stately corridors. The wildly-gleaming eyes, the capricious motions, the incoherent words around her, filled Lilian with terrified pity, with aching compassion. At every step her distress increased. She strove against it. She would not yield to it. She compelled herself to listen to the learned, benevolent physician who was conducting them. She strove in vain. The walls seemed curtained with sinister fantasies; chill ripples of fear shuddered along the pavement. The gliding presence behind pressed ever closer and closer. It seemed to touch her. Lilian paused.

"I can go no farther," she said. "I will wait here until you return."

The party passed on. The sound of their steps and of their voices died away. Lilian was left alone with the attendant, — a black-veiled nun.

"Shall I not bring you a glass of water, Signora?" said the nun, approaching her. "You look pale?"

"No, many thanks, my sister," replied Lilian. "But do not go. Stay by me. Will you not talk to me a little. Tell me something about these who are in your care. Which are the gentlest? Which do you love the best?"

"Ah, dear lady, I love them all. But there are two whom I pity the most. Do you see opposite that young girl walking up and down, looking in every corner? That is poor Teresita."

" What is she trying to find? "

" She is seeking her little sister. One day she took the child far among the hills for a walk. The child got tired of gathering flowers, and wanted to play at hide-and-seek. Teresita did as it wished, for it was her darling. Their mother was dead, and she had the whole care of it. The little thing hid at length, so that Teresita could not find it. She looked all the afternoon, she looked all the night. When she did not come home with the child, her father went in search of them. His neighbors joined him. They found Teresita the next morning. They never found the child. Whether it had wandered into some cave and could not make its way out, or whether the banditti had carried it off, no one knows. After that Teresita would do nothing but look after her little sister. There was no use in locking her up. She always got away and was found among the hills. So they brought her here."

Her fears forgotten in sympathy, Lilian rose and approached the cell. As the girl perceived her she sprang forward, clasping her hands.

" Oh Signora, have you seen her; have you

seen my little Beppa?" And, with a look of anguished entreaty, she fixed her large, imploring eyes on Lilian.

Lilian's throat swelled. She shook her head and turned away.

"Will she ever recover?" she asked of the nun.

"When little Beppa is found, Signora. Never till then. But will you not look at the other. She will not mind it. She takes notice of nothing."

Lilian followed the nun towards another door. Through the grate, she saw against the light from the narrow window the form of a young woman. She sat with her head bent down, her hands folded together.

Lilian gazed compassionately upon the attenuated outlines, the sad, downcast head.

The figure slowly raised its hands, and pressed them to its forehead.

The loose sleeves fell back.

Large white scars were on the arms.

Lilian put forth both hands and clutched the iron grating. Conscious only of one universal horror, she bent her eyes upon the figure.

Slowly it turned its head towards her.

She saw what seemed the ghost of Mira.

Lilian neither thought nor felt. In that moment the link between her soul and her body seemed to snap asunder.

She turned to the nun. She heard herself say that she could not wait for her party, that she must return at once. She knew that she was passing along the corridors and through the halls, that she entered the carriage, and ordered the servants to drive to the palazzo. She sat rigid and upright. Her perceptions seemed to absorb her whole force. The sunlight blazed into her brain. The various noises of the street sounded close upon her ear. The motion of the carriage jarred her every nerve.

She reached her home. As she ascended the staircase, the sense of all that was began to come upon her. She gained her apartments, her own room. She stood in the middle of the floor. She looked upward. She said one word.

" God."

That one appeal !

Then she opened her desk. She took out her purse and her letter of credit. She was ready. All that remained was to write to him. She seated herself. She wrote. She sealed the lines, directed them, laid them on her table.

She felt cold. She shivered. On the sofa lay a large shawl, her grandmother's parting gift. She wrapt it about her.

As if borne up, not touching the ground, she passed through the vacant rooms, down the staircase, into the street. She drew her veil closely around her, and walked rapidly on until she met an empty vettura. She signed to the driver. He stopped. She entered the carriage.

"Dove, Signora?"

"To the steamboat for Civita Vecchia."

She was driven to the quay. She reached the vessel. A few moments of strange voices and strange faces, and she found herself alone in a state-room.

She did not think. She could not think. One idea rose above all others. "When would the vessel leave?" On that one idea her mind hung, it pressed.

The sunlight streamed in through the small window and lay in a square, bright patch before her. It seemed a living thing looking at her. "When would the vessel leave?"

At length a prolonged hissing, as of a mighty serpent, came through the window. The vessel shook, the wheels revolved, slowly at first, then faster, faster. She was going. It was bearing her away. She started to her feet. The agony was coming.

"God, God, help me, God, to bear it."

As one who in the struggle of death grasps the holy cross, so Lilian clung to the Presence above her. She dared not remember. She dared not look forward. She sat through the long night, half benumbed, yet quivering each instant as from a dagger's stroke, silently, ceaselessly repeating, "Help me, God, to bear it."

---*---

LXI.

THE long night passed. The gray dawn crept noiselessly into the state-room, touching with cold fingers every projecting point, gliding among the shadows, silently warning them away. They paled, they disappeared. The first day of Lilian's widowhood — worse than widowhood — had begun.

The jerking pulsation of the steamboat ceased. Harsh, rattling sounds, mixed with the trampling of feet, came from above. The vessel had reached the port.

Lilian rose. Her knees bent under her. Holding by the wood-work, she gained the door, opened it, and ascended the staircase.

The deck was crowded. There was hurrying to and fro, the sound of many voices, and the glaring of the sun. Everything looked strange and dislocated to her. The voices seemed at an unnatural pitch ; the faces wore exaggerated expressions. She felt like a bodiless phantom, without any common tie of humanity connecting her with those around. Every motion she made, every word she uttered, was by a separate effort of volition, as she passed through the necessary formalities, — was rowed to the shore, and placed herself in a vettura.

Again across the bleak waste of the Campagna. Again towards the Silent City, the City of the Departed, — meet shelter for her whose song of thanksgiving was silenced, the life of whose life lay dead.

The long bright day unrolled its cheerless pageant of sunny skies and snowy clouds above her. Lilian looked with an incredulous eye around. Was it indeed the same world on which yesterday's sun had risen ? What was she yesterday ? Where, what was she now ?

Memories bitterer than death pursued her.

Rushes of uncontrollable thought swept over her. The past floated like a shrouded phantom before her. It was leading her back to the Silent City, to the convent, still, deathlike, the home of Sorrow, the chosen dwelling of Grief, her fittest refuge now.

The day wore on. The unnatural tension of Lilian's brain began to yield to exhaustion. Objects seemed slipping from the grasp of her mind. Her thoughts receded indefinitely before her. She sought in vain to pursue them, to hold them. They faded from her, and lost themselves in mist. Gradually all her perceptions merged themselves in the sense of motion. Rocked by the swaying of the carriage, Lilian slept.

Uprooted from the pleasant garden of her life, torn from the loving shelter of her home, adrift on the cold waves, she was borne unconscious on towards the unknown future, veiled in impenetrable shadow, mantled with blackest night.

Lilian was aroused by the carriage-door being thrown open.

"Siamo arrivati, Signora. Eccoci alla locanda," said the rough, good-natured voice of the vetturino.

A servant of the hotel came forward. Lilian asked if she could have rooms.

"I don't know if there are any rooms free, Signora," said the man, scanning her with an inquisitive eye. "I will ask the padrona."

He disappeared within, and presently returned, following a large, portly woman, with cold, black eyes, and harshly-marked features.

"I am sorry, Madama," she began, as she advanced to the carriage-door. She checked herself, as her glance fell upon the costly folds of Eastern fabric, which enveloped the stranger. "Quanto è bestia quel domestico!" she muttered to herself; and, with fluent greeting, she begged Lilian to descend.

"Has the Signora any orders?" she asked, as she ushered Lilian into a large, well-furnished, desolate-looking room.

"Do you know Dr. Albertazzi's address?"

"Certainly, Signora; he is here just beside us, in the next piazza."

"I wish him to come this evening, or to-morrow morning as early as possible."

The hostess retired.

The tall candles on the mantel-piece shed an uncertain light through the room. The ticking of the clock had a solemn, warning sound. Nothing else broke the silence. Life seemed to stand still, listening to the passing of time.

A knock came at the door. It opened, and the young daughter of the hostess entered.

"Il Signor dottore is not at home, Signora. The servant waited long for his return, but when it grew so late, he left the message for to-morrow morning."

Lilian bowed her head.

The weary, woe-stamped face, the hopeless look in the stranger's eyes as she turned them upon the girl, sank into her heart. With the impulsive sympathy of her race, she recognized a great grief; with feminine tact, she spoke.

"The Signora is fatigued, — but the Signora has forgotten that she has eaten nothing. If the Signora will allow me to serve her myself." And without awaiting an answer, she left the room.

For more than twenty-four hours, Lilian had not tasted food. She would gladly have never eaten again. There was something inexpressibly repugnant in the idea of again returning to the daily routine of life, after the shock, the wrench from all that made life dear to her. Why should she eat? Why should she seek to live? It were better to die and be at rest, — gently to glide down the last descent, to find forgetfulness and sleep below.

A sense of faintness came over her. She rose and threw back the window. Before her lay the broad, overshadowed piazza. The soft rays of the rising moon rested upon the summit of the great Egyptian obelisk, which stood pointing from amid the darkness below, its unwearied finger to Heaven. Beneath, from the gloom which wrapt its base, came the restless flow of unseen fountains, dashing impatiently, foaming unceasingly, like the desires of men chafing against the boundaries of fate. And still unmoved, unwavering, steady amid the strife, the ancient stone fulfilled its mandate, ever pointing upward, bearing mute witness to the Power above.

As Lilian gazed, the teaching of the silent monument came to her in deep, soundless tones, nerving her once more to raise the burden of her life.

" Patience, oh mourners. Yet a little while, and ye shall cease to be. Your eyes shall weep no more, your hearts no longer ache. Faith! ye afflicted. At the end ye shall read tho beginning. What is hidden shall be revealed, what is dark, made clear. Look upward. Faint not. He to whom I point, He careth for you."

LXII.

" IL Signor dottore Albertazzi."

A shiver ran over Lilian at the name of the frequent, ever-welcome guest of the winter before. It passed and left her marble still. She rose to meet him.

" Mrs. Clinton, what has happened? " he exclaimed abruptly, as his eye flashed over her rigid face, her unyielding form.

In tones as rigid as her features Lilian spoke.

" His wife is not dead. She is in Naples. I wish to live in a convent. Will you help me ? "

A dark glow overspread the swarthy countenance of the Italian.

" But this is too dreadful ! " burst from him.

Lilian's face did not alter. No self-pity softened her eyes, dilated as by some ever-present memory of horror. Her whole frame was strained to endure.

Dr. Albertazzi walked up and down the room. He returned and sat down near the still, pale form.

" I have no words. Let me serve you if I can."

Lilian did not speak.

" You have no near relations? "

" None."

" You are here alone? "

She bowed her head. Each moment she grew more rigid. She seemed stiffening into stone. The Italian rose.

" I shall soon return. I go to make the arrangements you desire."

Lilian silently placed in his hand her letter of credit.

He looked a moment on the marble face. His chest tightened. He could not speak. What speech could reach the unapproachable isolation of such a sorrow.

" You will write," she hardly articulated.

He bowed reverently and went out, softly closing the door behind him. The daughter of the hostess met him.

" Ah Signore dottore, what is it? What has happened to the lady? "

" A great calamity, figlia mia."

" May I slip into the room to sit in the corner and wait on her? "

" No. She had better be alone."

LIII.

THE sun had set ere the Italian returned. " I
have been gone a long time. There was much
to be done before I could obtain the permissions
I desired for you. You are received as an in-
mate, but exempted from obedience to the convent rules, and you are allowed to wear the nun's
habit."

Lilian rose.

" Can I go now ? "

" The carriage is waiting."

He gave her his arm and conducted her towards the staircase. The daughter of the hostess
met them. She caught Lilian's hand, raised it
to her lips and burst into tears.

Lilian turned an impassive eye upon the girl.
A vague surprise passed through her thoughts.
She could not weep for herself. Why should
others weep for her ?

In the gathering twilight, past the palaces, the
fountains, the churches, the monuments, through
the dark-winding streets, the dim, wide piazzas,
Lilian was driven. They entered the ruins. Past
temples once glad with song of sacrifice and joyful hymns, now shattered and ruined; arches

raised by jubilant conquerors across the crowded streets of the imperial city, now spanning solitary scarce-trodden ways; ruins of towering piles, majestic palaces, their stately halls now open to the wind, their waiting crowds, their thousand slaves, all gone, all vanished into nothingness; — past ancient Rome they held their way towards a solitary, time-worn pile, rising high above its storied terraces of green.

They passed up the grass-grown steps, and entered the dark shadow cast by the convent wall. Lilian's guide stopped at a low door. He knocked; it opened, and a veiled figure, holding a lamp, appeared standing in the ghostly moonlight of the inner court.

"I must not enter," said the Italian. "Farewell."

The door closed upon Lilian. She stood alone with the black-veiled nun in the stone-paved court; before her the heavy walls and small grated windows of the convent. No sound broke the death-like silence, save the hooting of an owl from the neighboring ruins.

She followed the black, stoled figure, as it entered the building, and passed along a narrow passage, up a winding staircase of stone, to an oaken door.

23 *

The nun knocked, and entered alone. She returned, and bade Lilian advance.

She found herself in a small but lofty room. The iron lamp that hung from the ceiling shed its light upon a tall, spare figure, with sunken cheeks and deep, black eyes, whose fire seemed to have been long ago quenched in tears.

"It is the abbess, — kneel," whispered her conductress; and Lilian mechanically obeyed.

"Be blessed, my daughter, and now arise," said a calmly commanding voice.

Lilian arose. The nun had disappeared. She was alone with the abbess, the tortured Christ looking down on her from the great ebony crucifix.

"Daughter, sorely wounded you have come to the abode of peace. May God's comfort breathe upon you; may Christ's healing descend upon you; may the Holy Mother's pity console you. Go in peace, my daughter. Watch and pray, and wait."

Like snowflakes on the dark wintry waters, so softly fell the clear, pure tones on Lilian's soul. The iron band that had been closing around her seemed to relax its clasp. The voice unlocked the frozen fountains of her heart. Tears rose to her dark, dilated eyes, but sank to their bed again.

The abbess rang a small bell on a table beside

her. The nun again appeared. Lilian followed, walking as in a dream, the gliding figure and the glimmering lamp, through hushed corridors and moonlit galleries, until they paused at a narrow door. The nun opened it. The moonlight streamed within, marking the lines of the barred window on the stone floor, showing the low pallet, the wooden chair and table, which were the only furniture of the cell. On the bed lay the black robes of a nun.

" Good-night, Signora."

The door closed, the retreating footsteps died along the corridor, and Lilian was left alone.

She turned an affrighted glance around the narrow cell. She stretched out her arms with sudden motion.

" Harvey ! "

As the despairing cry reëchoed from the cold walls, Lilian sank, sank she knew not whither.

The shadow of the grated window moved slowly over the prostrate figure, the deathlike face. Life held aloof, as loath to lay again its heavy burden on that much-tried heart; till, through the night and stillness, mournfully pealing, came the sound of the convent-bell. Its vibrations throbbed through the darkened chambers of her brain, and summoned her to life. Shuddering, she arose, and laid herself on the low pallet.

The sound of opening doors, the sweeping of garments, the measured tread of feet, mingled with the close resounding summons. They ceased, and all was still, when, softly swelling through the silence, came the chanted prayer.

"God, great Father, hear us! From the strife of life, from the beating of the tempest, from the tossing of the waves, hither have we fled. Send down Thy blessing on us! Grant us Thy peace!

"Christ, Holy One, oh, hear us! Thou who didst bear our life, Thou who didst weep for us, Thou who didst die for us, send down Thy blessing on us! Grant us Thy peace!

"Virgin, Spotless Mother, hear us! Thou who didst stand while the sword pierced through thy soul, whilst in his agony thy dear Son did hang upon the cross, send down thy blessing on us! Grant us thy peace!"

The simple, ancient words, the chorussed voices, the pealing of the organ, in earnest invocation, breathed through the midnight air. Over the ruins of the antique world without, over the sadder ruins of human hopes within, they sounded in their sweet solemnity.

God seemed nearer to Lilian.

Surely He heard that prayer.

LXIV.

As some glad stream which flows rejoicing on, between its velvet banks of sunny green, reflecting fair things sweet and beautiful, — the drooping boughs of overhanging trees, the tender hues of slender-stemmèd flowers, the flush of morn, the glory of the eve, the far-off splendor of the midnight stars, — and sings, sings ever of its happiness, — then sinks at once into deep, dreadful caves, far from the sweet sun and the scented air, far from the rippling joy of its clear course, far from the song of birds, the breath of flowers, and, dumb with grief, glides through those murky halls, beneath whose silent vaults no life is found, struck into Death-Land by one moment's plunge, void of all hope, a river of Despair, — so Lilian's life, wrenched from its happy course, flowed on within the silent convent-walls. Patient and still and sad, she glided through the shaded corridors, her dark robes, like the shadow of her fate, enfolding her young life and love with a funereal pall; or paced the worn stones of the cloister walk, where slender shafts of carved and twisted stone upheld the arches of the light-hung roof; tracing their shadows on the graven slabs, that told the name of many a buried nun, life's trouble over, resting in her grave. And Lilian would stand with folded hands, and read the scanty record of their lives, and wonder if among them there had been one, only one, as wretched as herself.

Or she would wander listlessly amid the tangled paths of the old garden waste, and sit by ruined fountains, listening, with dreaming ear, the faint, complaining flow of waters trickling from their shattered vase, and winding under thickets of dim shade, mournfully murmuring as they stole away.

She would stray between the green walls, 'neath the arching boughs of laurel walks, where ceaseless twilight·reigned; and if a struggling sunbeam wandered thróugh, it gleamed up starlike from the path ·below. Safe from all harmful wile and snare cf man, the little birds sang from those shadowy groves, making sweet music .all the livelong day. The nightingale, unmindful of the sun, poured forth in those sequestered halls her notes, sighing forth softness in luxurious chant. Sweet hypo-crite, feigning an unfelt woe so fair, that tears would gush from the full heart of the sad human listener, the while the little songstress plained at joyful ease.

Broad lawns and sloping banks and terraced sweeps would woo her slow and half-unconscious step; and spreading shade of solemn whispering oak, and moonlight olive, would invite to rest. Red poppies flamed amid the soft, green grass, mixed with large snowy bells and purple sprays, and untrained roses waved their fragrant blooms, and flung out sweetness on the lonely air. No hand reproved the wild luxuriance, no careful watch restrained their wayward will; flowers sprang daring from the gravelled paths, and climbed in sport around the ancient trees. The ivy wound about blank pedestals, and twined around the gray-flecked marble forms, the only guardians of that solitude, binding their limbs in trembling verdant chains.

Upon an open sweep a dial lay, fringed by tall grasses and by feathery ferns, spotted by white and stained with yellow moss. No guiding shadow touched its hours with life; it lay and looked up blankly at the sun, — a vacant, useless, and for-gotten stone, its duties past, its very memory gone. It had a mournful charm for Lilian. Oft would she come and kneel beside it there, and think how like·her life that dial was. She grew to love its cold, unconscious face. She almost felt that it could feel for her.

When the vibrating summons of the bell rang through the cloisters, floating forth across the peaceful garden wilderness below, to lose itself among the ruined piles, and o'er the silent, sunny plain beyond, then Lilian·would join the sisterhood, and kneel beside them in their place of prayer, and lift with theirs her sweet, young voice to Heaven, praying for help to bear her Father's will with gentle patience and unmurmuring thought, for mercy to be strengthened to endure, and courage to look forward to the end, — praying for him she never more might see, –- for him, the husband of one happy year, loved even more in that slow agony than in the gladness of their joyous days, — praying for her, the heavily-smitten one, the tender, loving sister of her youth, Mira, the guiltless cause of so much woe, the wife sore wounded with unconscious wrong. The dim light fell athwart the painted panes in glowing harmonies of fervent tones, and rested on the rows of black-veiled forms, their hands clasped suppliant to the Christ, who smiled in infant sweetness from the altar-piece; and, leaning from his gentle mother's arms, held in his dimpled hand, towards those ranks of kneeling worshippers, the mystic branch of olive, — pledge of peace serene, assured, peace that no cruel hand can wrench away, — the peace of God, that passeth understanding.

So, pacing o'er the monumental stones, the graven pavement of the cloister aisles; gliding amid the verdurous, starry shade, sitting beside the sadly-trickling founts, resting beneath the solemn, spreading trees, kneeling beside the quiet sisterhood, her fair face gleaming from her sable robes, like a white lily shining from a bier, her long, still days passed on.

———◆———

LXV.

LILIAN's sorrow was too overwhelming to allow of passionate outbreak. Its immensity had crushed out of her will the impulse to resist. She could not even wish relief, for life, — sacred; beloved life, — stood between her and the ceasing of her wretchedness. God's hand was laid upon her, and by its weight she knew that it was God's. The very excess of her misery brought one consolation with it. She felt the more His love. It was her only refuge. It was all she had. All else had failed her. God would never fail her. In the

24

darkness and silence of the night, she would lift up her thoughts from out the mournful solitude, and pray, and feel her prayer raise her to the Eternal Arms; and soothed, consoled, and comforted, she would rest in the pitying bosom of her Father, and sink to sleep.

As time wore on, she learned to place the idea of God as a shield between her and her memories. It was her duty to abjure remembrance. Her happiness, innocent in itself, recalled with longing, would taint her soul with sin. Not only the future, not only the present, God demanded of her the past. And she sealed solemnly the memory of her wedded love, and offered it with aching obedience. And God received the sacrifice. He placed it among His precious things. He looked upon her, and blessed her with His grace. He sent down the sweetness of His spirit, and breathed upon her soul. She was no more alone. She walked with God. His hand gently upheld her daily steps, and gave to her lips draughts of those living waters of which whoever drinks shall thirst no more.

LXVI.

Lilian stood at the grated window of her cell, and looked down on the grassy quadrangle below, closed in by the graceful arches of the shaded cloisters. From time to time, a little bird would dart across the open space, and the yellow wall-flowers nod·to each other. Nothing else moved.

A joyful bark, a burst of girlish laughter, sounded along the cloister-wall, startling the silent echoes into jocund life. Into the checkered sun-light sprang the figure of a girl, chased by a little dog. Her robe of purple silk, her golden orna-ments, flashed into alternate brightness, and sank into intervening shadow, as she danced over the worn tombstones and frolicked around the sculp-tured shafts, hiding, reappearing, pursuing, and fleeing, while her ever-returning laughter made glad music on the wondering air.

Lilian gazed in pleased surprise on the joyous apparition, as it flitted in its happy merriment around the solemn shades, making their twilight radiant with the gladness of its youth.

At length, as if weary of sport, the girl called to the little dog, took it in her arms, and seated herself on the edge of the cloister, between the shafts of stone. She turned her face upwards. Her eye rested upon Lilian, standing, with folded hands, at the grated window. She sprang to her feet, dropping the astonished dog, gazed up for a

moment, then, followed by her indjgnantly bark-
ing little companion, bounded into the cloister,
and disappeared.

Springing footsteps echoed along the gallery,
mingled with the hurried pattering of paws. A
knock sounded at the door.

" Entrate."

It opened, and the apparition of the cloisters
below darted within, a girl of childish features,
but rounded figure, sparkling, glittering,. smiling,
fresh, — the very counterpart of joyous Spring.

Lilian stood in silent astonishment.

" You are the English sister, are you not? "
said the girl.

" They call me so."

" I knew you were, for they said she was young
and beautiful. Keep still, Tomm ; what are you
about ? "

The dog, a purple Isle of Skye terrier, was
standing on its hind legs, and impatiently claim-
ing Lilian's attention. She stooped and patted
its head. It sniffed, and licked her hand. Tears
started to Lilian's eyes. It was the first caress
she had received for many months. She looked
gratefully at the dumb creature with its large,
intelligent eyes. They recalled to her the lov-

ing gaze of Great Heart, — Great Heart resting
in dreamless slumber under the great tree below
her little garden in that far-off land.

"Do come down into the garden with me,"
said the girl coaxingly. "I have been here two
hours, and I am so lonely already that I don't
know what to do with myself. I can't play with
Tomm all day long, though he is a darling," and
she caught up the terrier and printed a strenuous
kiss upon his mop-like head. "Will you come?"

Lilian turned silently towards the door. She
had so seldom spoken of late that she expressed
her assent by gesture rather than by words.

Along the dark corridor with its hundred
doors, down the winding staircase, through the
shaded cloisters, Lilian followed the flitting footsteps of her companion, who chatted the while gayly
with the little dog, ever and anon looking back to
assure herself of the English sister's presence.

As they entered the garden, the girl clapped her
hands together and bounded forward with her dog.
Lilian stood and watched the gracefully circling
figure, listening to the gay laughter as one listens to a foreign language, sweet to the ear, but
incomprehensible to the sense. Returning as
quickly as she had sped away, the girl took Lil-

ian's hand, drew her to a shady bank, and cast
herself at her feet, looking up into her face.

"How beautiful you are! You are as beautiful as the Beatrice that hangs in my horrid old
uncle's palace. And you look something like her,
only not so despairing. Did you ever see that
picture?"

Lilian bowed her head. She had seen it many
times in that loved companionship, — and now —

"Is it possible that you are cold? How can
any one shiver in this sun! Won't you run a
little with Tomm and warm yourself? No?"

The sunlight that fell in golden streams through
the dividing branches of the great tree above,
struck on Lilian's face and showed the sharp contraction of pain.

"I hope I haven't said anything to trouble
you," said the girl anxiously. "My aunt would
be much displeased if I did. She told me that I
might ask you to come into the garden with me.
I am glad you are here. It will be so much pleas-
anter."

"Surely you are not going to take the veil?"
said Lilian.

"Oh no. I am making my retreat for the
month before I am married, as all the women of

my family do. And besides, my aunt won't receive any one who has not a true vocation. Have you not seen how different the sisters here are from those in other convents?"

"I know nothing of other convents," replied Lilian.

"They are not nice places at all. The nuns are made to take the veil against their will more than half the time, and they are so stupid and so greedy, it's quite shocking. And they are asleep almost all the time that they are at prayers, and they are always spying and telling tales about each other. When we were at Florence last year, mamma fell ill and they sent me to a convent to get me out of the way. I was quite disgusted with every one there. This is very different, but I can't say that I like even this. I come once a year for a month, and I find it a great *seccatura*, though I love my aunt dearly."

"The abbess?" inquired Lilian.

"Yes. I love her all the more because she has had so much to suffer. Do you know about her?"

Lilian shook her head.

"She was the eldest daughter. There were two brothers and two sisters. The family was not rich, and the parents had decided that the daughters should go into a convent, so that the sons might have everything for themselves. My aunt was very beautiful and very gay, and cheerful. She never wanted to go into a convent, and at length she fell in love with a young man, a friend of her brother's, and then of course she was perfectly miserable at the idea of being made a nun. The young man told her parents that he would marry her without any dowry, but they said that such a thing had never happened in the family as a daughter's being married without a dowry, and that it could not be. She wept and prayed, but they were resolved that she should go into a convent. When she saw that she could not prevail on them, she ran away with her lover. Nobody knows much about that part. The only thing I could ever make out was that they were pursued and overtaken, and that she was carried at once to the convent, — this convent, — and that the eldest brother fought a duel with the lover and killed him. When she knew that her lover was dead, for six months she never spoke a word. She fasted and prayed till all her beauty was gone, and she did such dreadful penances that the Cardinal had to interfere and forbid them. And when the abbess died, she was made abbess. When she was abbess, whenever a novice presented herself, she had a private conversation with her, and if she found that the girl had not a proper, heavenly vocation, she refused her, and sent word to all the other convents of her being refused for want of a true vocation, and then none of the other convents dared to receive her, for this convent is known to be the holiest in Rome.

"After she had been abbess some time, her parents wanted to make my mother, who was a great many years younger, a nun. They thought that of course she would receive her own sister. But my aunt had a private conversation with her, just as with all the rest, and she refused her, and sent word to all the other convents of her being refused, and so my mother was married as she wanted to be. You can imagine how she loves my aunt, and so we all do. None of us would do anything that she disapproved of for the world."

"Then she approves your marriage?" said Lilian, interest in the beautiful child-woman beginning to stir within her.

"Oh, yes. She never kissed me so tenderly nor held me so close as when I was called in to be told about it after it was decided upon."

"And you love him?" asked Lilian.

The girl's eyes sparkled, her cheeks flushed, her lips parted with a quick smile.

" Look," she said. And as if the sight of her lover's face were the most conclusive answer, she drew from her bosom a miniature, and placed it in Lilian's hand.

It was the portrait of a very young man, with the regular features, the attenuated and receding chin, and the carefully curled hair which distinguish the young Italian nobles of the present day. There was a smile of courteous affability on the lips, the eyes were soft, the bearing high-bred.

" Is he not beautiful ? " said the girl, as her eyes dwelt lovingly upon the portrait. " And he is so amiable ! His mother and sisters perfectly idolize him. They write me such letters about him. They say that I shall find him much handsomer than his portrait."

" What, have you never seen him ? " asked Lilian, startled into surprise.

" No. But I have his picture and his letters and his poetry, and that is quite enough to love him with. We shall be married in four weeks, and then I shall see him all the time, you know." And the girl lay contentedly back on the grass and contemplated the portrait until the bell summoned them to the chapel-prayers.

LXVII.

LILIAN sat by the sun-dial. She sat and looked and wondered. From the fracture which crossed the stone, just in its centre, grew a pale green stem. Slender and straight it reared itself, casting its shadow on the dial-plate. She could read the hours. No longer useless, hopeless, blank, — again a guide, an aid, a monitor, noting the silent moments as they passed, telling once more the preciousness of time, — the broken dial woke to life again.

Esmeralda came slowly from one of the dark laurel walks, disregardful of Tomm, who, alternately walking on his hind legs, and giving impatient jumps, with doggish blandishments, vainly invited her to a race over the glittering grass, and around the mossy trees.

She seated herself beside Lilian, and began absently to trace figures with her finger upon the dial. As she bent, a heavy tear-drop fell upon the stone.

" Has anything grieved you ? " inquired Lilian, solicitously.

" Yes. I have done something very unkind. I don't see how I could have forgotten ! Last month, I heard of a poor woman in great distress, and I promised to go and see her, and the very next day I heard that I was to be married, and I was so glad that I forgot all about her, and I have never remembered her till now. And here I am, shut up, and all the family have gone to Poggianone, and I have no one to send. I feel so sorry and so ashamed to have forgotten the suffering of others, because I was so happy myself."

" To have forgotten the suffering of others, because I was so unhappy myself!" So an inaudible voice repeated the words to Lilian's inner ear.

She turned her face upward to the sky. A new thought rose within her, and glorified the sunlight. In tones of remembered sweetness, the morning song of the birds came to her ear. A new, a glad perception opened before her. A new love extended wide its world-embracing arms.

Under the Russian snows, there grows a plant of shining foliage and of crimson fruit. In the cold night of winter, it steals up from the frozen ground. Under the white-spread desolation it ripens. Its leaves are polished like the victor palm, its berries ruby as with the earth's heart blood. Even so had Lilian's winter of grief ripened celestial fruit. Suffering had brought forth resignation. From resignation was springing a still nobler birth. In harmonious development, gently, tenderly was she led up the steps of our mortal ascent, towards the perfection of an universal love.

"I will go," she said.

"Will you? Can you? Oh, yes, I remember my aunt said that you were exempted from the rules, because you had made so great a donation to the poor. I am so glad. I should have had no peace. I will run to my aunt, and get money."

"I had rather you went to my cell," said Lilian. "You will find my purse there."

The girl returned. Talking gayly, she accompanied Lilian through the stone-paved courtyard to the postern-gate.

As Lilian descended the grass-grown steps of the broad terraces, the sense of isolation pressed upon her overpoweringly. She felt an all but irresistible impulse to turn back and seek again the shelter of the convent walls. The sunlight seemed strange and unfriendly. The unwalled space distressed her. She felt bewildered. She gazed around. Her eye rested upon the Colosseum. On such a brilliant day as this, she had first beheld it with him. Before her rose that manly presence and that noble face. She saw again the smile of those serious eyes; she heard once more the deep-toned cadence of his voice. Lilian sank on the lowest step, and groaned aloud. She had not the strength. How could she go on into that outer world, so filled with the bitterness of pain! But her errand. She must not turn back. She would not look, she would not raise her eyes, but her errand must be done.

Along the solitary road, past the ruins, through the narrow streets, stilling her rushing thoughts as best she might, steadily, with downcast eyes, not daring to look up, she held her way towards her destination. She reached the house, and entered the dark portal. Up the worn, winding staircase, she passed, she gained the door which Esmeralda had indicated. She knocked. A faint voice bade her enter. She crossed the threshold. Want, Woe, and Sickness met her face to face.

On a bed, the only article of furniture in the room, save one broken chair, lay a woman. Her black eyes looked out with a haggard stare from her colorless face; her lips were parted with the unbreathing look of utter hopelessness. By her side lay a child of about five years, pale and shrunken.

Lilian glided forward to the bedside.

" Tell me, my poor woman, what can I do for you ? "

The woman looked anxiously in her face.

" I am hungry," she whispered.

Lilian's heart turned sick.

" And the child ? "

" He has the fever. When I ask him, he says he does not want to eat."

Lilian bent over the child. He turned his little head away.

" Poverello mio, caro figliuolino, are you hungry ? "

The child made no reply.

" Is there nothing, nothing that you want ? "

He turned his face towards her.

" Yes, — an orange, but I can't have it."

" You shall have anything, everything," she exclaimed; and hastily descending the staircase, she passed into the street. She looked hurriedly around. She heard the sound of singing and dancing. In an adjacent courtyard, she saw, through the open gate, a circle of bold-eyed girls dancing la Forestiera, while some young men stood by, laughing and applauding. A witch-like old woman sat on the stones near her, leaning against the wall, twirling her distaff, and mum-

bling to herself. Lilian approached her; but, as
the hag raised her eyes, they wore such an. expression of malice, that she recoiled. A woman,
nursing a baby, and scolding two little children,
who were quarrelling together, was the only other
being in sight.

Lilian passed down the roughly-paved street,
directing her steps towards the fountain of Trevi.
She reached the small, crowded piazza. Women
were drawing water in their tapering, broad-
based copper vases; contadini were loitering and
jesting at the little stalls; children were selling
violets; itinerant venders were filling the air with
their discordant cries; the carriages of strangers
were driving slowly past, or stopping before the
tumbling, foaming, broad-spread torrent. The
Tritons blew their horns and lashed their finny
tails. All was tumult and noisy confusion in that
one busy, restless place of quiet, silent Rome.

Lilian threaded her way through the crowd.
She entered a shop. A large, cheerful-eyed woman sat behind the counter.

" Good-day, my sister," said the mistress, rising. " What can I do for you ? "

" There is a woman, starving, near by. I want
food and help at once."

" Santa Vergine, what things people do hear ! Ah, the poor find it harder than ever, nowadays. Here, Mariuccia ! " she called.

" A brown-skinned, ruddy-cheeked peasant appeared from the dusky, inner doorway.

" Quick, take some soup from the *marmita* and a half loaf of bread, and follow the sister."

Lilian took up some of the oranges and grapes which were placed amid the dainty cakes and delicate confections on the counter. She drew forth her purse.

" Oh no, my sister, — not from a nun ! "

Lilian silently laid down a coin and left the shop, followed by the maid. Her heart beat quick, her step was elastic. She took no heed of the passers, the fountain, the manifold memories of the place, once her favorite moonlight resort. A sensation of joy, almost of happiness ran through her, as she sprang up the dark stone steps, entered the narrow room, and gave the golden orange and cooling grapes into the child's hot hand. The little creature gave a cry of delight. Eagerly it pressed its parched lips on the fruit.

Forgetting her hunger, the mother leaned over it.

" Is it good, my blessed angel ? " she said with a tearful smile.

" Oh, so good, and so good!" answered the child in the expressive Italian idiom.

Lilian gave Dr. Albertazzi's address to the maid, and placed some silver in her hand. I wish him to come at once."

The child finished the fruit she had given. It turned restlessly from side to side. The mother sought in vain to quiet it. Lilian rose and drew near. She held out her hands. " Will you not come and sit with me a little while, you will feel so nice and fresh and cool ? "

The child looked at her a moment, undecided, then stretched out its arms. She seated herself on the broken chair, resting its head upon her bosom. Gradually the child pressed its head back to her arm, and lay, its look fixed on the sweet face above, with the open-eyed gaze, so preternaturally intelligent which we see, — those are happy who have never seen it, — in the eyes of a sick child. An expression of gentle quietude dawned on the wasted little face. The child turned its head towards Lilian and lay quite still.

A step ascended the staircase. The door opened and Dr. Albertazzi entered. A smile played around his firmly cut mouth and softened the keen glance of his eye as it rested upon Lilian.

"I am glad to meet you here," he said, as he looked around. "You were needed."

"The mother was starving, I fear, and the child has the fever." And Lilian bent anxiously over the shrunken little form.

The physician advanced to the bedside.

"Ebbene, my poor woman, what is it?"

"I had no work, no money, no food."

"Coraggio. The lady," he corrected himself, "the sister will see that you have work as soon as you are fit for it. And the child?"

"The fever."

"A few doses of quinine and proper nursing will soon bring him right," said the physician, as he examined the little creature, who moaned the while and nestled closer to Lilian. "Now I will go to the hospital and bring a sister to take care of him to-night."

"Can I not?" asked Lilian, a tone of disappointment in her voice.

"Not at night, the neighborhood is a villainous one. I will return with her." And he left the room.

The sun was sinking. The dusty column of light which streamed in through the small, high window was beginning to pale, as the physician again entered the room, followed by a nun.

" I will take the child, sister," she said, offering to relieve Lilian of her burden.

The child raised its head, looked at her, and pushed her away.

" I want this one," he said.

" To-morrow," said Lilian, gently disengaging herself from the child's clasp.

As she descended the staircase, she heard the child's wail — " I want the other," and the voice of the nun again promising, " To-morrow."

Again the cup of human love was held to Lilian's lips. Not as erst, sparkling with the golden flush of joy, but a cup of crimson vintage, watered by many tears, — such as good men have drunk of since the sun first trod his solemn path above this troublous earth.

LXVIII.

Lilian sat beneath one of the ruined arches of the Colosseum. The ancient walls rose in high and wide circles to meet the canopy of the deep blue sky. No footsteps echoed within those silent limits, no human voice disturbed the soli-

tude. She sat beneath the shade, — her black
robes sweeping around her in heavy folds, her
fair face looking forth from her snowy coif and
sable veil,— serene and steadfast. Her hands were
folded in still repose. She sat and communed with
the spirits of the past. She often came into that
holy place to find companionship and consolation
in the sainted air; to breathe in courage from the
mystic consecration sealed by the blood of martyrs.

A party entered the ruins, and chatting gayly,
approached the spot where she was seated. They
paused to look around.

" How much that nun looks like the beautiful
Mrs. Clinton," said a lady.

" What Mrs. Clinton," asked her attendant, —
a young man.

" Mrs. Harvey Clinton."

" I can't see the likeness. Mrs. Harvey Clinton is a blonde."

" Oh, no. You are quite mistaken," said another voice.

" I don't see how I can be mistaken. I saw
her two months ago, on the Nile. She was on
his arm, walking up and down the deck of their
boat; ours was along-side. She was very fair and
fragile looking, and she had deep blue eyes and
golden hair."

“ There must have been some mistake. It could not have been Harvey Clinton that you met.”

“ But I know him as well as I do you. He was thin and haggard-looking enough, but as polite and considerate as ever. To be sure, he did not ask us on his boat; but he sent us a quantity of wine, — we were almost out, — saying that he had no use for it.”

“ Oh, that explains it,” said another of the party, laughing. “ Now we see why it is that you brought away such a confused idea of Mrs. Clinton’s appearance.”

Laughing merrily, the party passed on.

Lilian pressed her hands over her eyes, and sat without moving, while pangs, sharper than those which rent the martyrs, racked her through and through.

Was there no way in which she could fulfil her daily mission of mercy, and yet escape the anguish of contact with the world ? Was there no hope, no refuge ? Suddenly, above the aching torrent of her thoughts, an idea rose, clear, distinct, illumined. The Hospital ! Yes, in those drear halls, sacred to Pain, the favorite haunt of Death, she could pass her life, unseen, unnoted, comforting the afflicted, ministering to those that mourn, smoothing the restless pillow of disease, soothing the pangs with which the body mourns the soul's departure. There was her appointed place. There would she go, and serve and watch and pray.

LXIX.

ANOTHER sister joined that patient band. A soft, light footstep trod the gloomy halls of the great Hospital; a low, gentle voice whispered its comfort to those impatient ears; a tender arm raised those aching heads; a sweet, pale face bent over those sad sufferers, cheering their sight as by the view of pure, untinted flowers.

Watching through the long, still hours of the night, kneeling by the dying, with solemn care draping the dead, serving, waiting, praying ever, she held her patient way.

Glorified by suffering, transfigured by pain, she dwelt as enfolded by the Invisible,—she walked in the light of the smile of God.

LXX.

LILIAN slept. She was awakened by the voice of a nun, who stood beside her, shading a lamp with her hand.

" I am grieved to wake you, sister; but a messenger has come, and asks for some one who
speaks English, if we have any such among us."

Lilian rose and dressed herself in haste. She
passed the dark corridors, and entered the great
vestibule. A servant stood waiting. " It is not
far, my sister," he said; and led the way through
the silent, half-lighted streets, towards a piazza,
its hundred steps and stone-wrought balustrades
shining brightly in the moonlight. Up the Sca-
linata they passed, and stood on the hill above,
the Silent City beneath them, the ancient church
and still more ancient obelisk before them, the
groves of the eminence stretching motionless away
towards the outer walls. A few steps brought
them to a lofty palazzo of dark-gray stone. The
great door opened at their approach, and Lilian
was ushered up a broad, thickly-carpeted staircase,
through richly-adorned saloons, into a large, dim,
heavily-curtained sleeping-room. A lamp glim-
mered from the hearth; the ticking of a clock
came from an adjoining apartment.

A tall, severe-looking woman rose and came
softly forward to meet Lilian. In a whisper, she
conveyed the directions for the night.

" I am sorry to.have to leave her; but I've

watched three nights, and my master will not allow me to take care of her, day and night, any longer. She's as gentle as a lamb. It's a pleasure to wait on her; but I feel easier about leaving her, now that I have seen you. I shall be on the couch in the dressing-room. If you want anything, you must call me. She is very, very ill."

She left the room through an open door. Lilian sat by the bed. The luxury around her, unseen since that one dreadful day which had taken from her her home, her name, her all, filled her mind with haunting memories. In such a home as this she had lived with him. In such —— No. She would not think. It was over. God had taken it from her.

The sound of a door carefully unclosed came from the dressing-room. She heard the voice of the maid. "She is asleep, Sir;" and the door closed softly again.

Lilian sat and watched, listening to the light, hurried breathing of the sleeper. At length she turned restlessly upon her pillow. Lilian rose and bent over her.

"Do you wish anything?"

"No. It is my head," she whispered; and she pressed her hands to her forehead.

Lilian laid her palm upon the hot, throbbing brow. The lady's hands fell back.

"How cool, how soft," she sighed.

Lilian stood silently beside her. The lady lay without moving. Only the quick, hurried breathing broke the silence, mingling with the ticking of the clock. At length she spoke.

"I fear I am very selfish. Are you not tired?"

"No," replied Lilian; "I often stand so all night."

"But will you not sit down?" And, moving with difficulty, she made place for Lilian beside her. "I cannot rest if I think you are weary."

"Can you not sleep again?" asked Lilian.

"I fear to sleep. I so often have dreadful dreams. And when I awake, I do not know if they are only dreams, or if they are true. Sometimes I think it is a dream that I am alive."

The veins of the temples beneath Lilian's touch began to beat hurriedly.

"Do not talk any more just now," she said, soothingly. "Will you not hold my other hand? It often happens that holding a hand brings quiet, dreamless sleep. Will you not try it?"

The hot, thin fingers felt in the twilight for the gentle hand, clasped it obediently, and the lady spoke no more.

The night wore on. Slowly the gray light stole through the parting curtains, shedding a dim, uncertain shadow through the room. Lilian still held her hand upon the sleeper's brow, the unconscious fingers still clasped hers.

The sense of a presence came over Lilian. The blood at her heart stopped. Her breath was suspended. Slowly she turned her head towards the door.

As if struck into stone, one hand holding back the heavy curtain of the doorway, his face white, his eyes riveted upon her, she saw Mr. Clinton.

A chill as of death crept over Lilian. She rose, her look fixed upon him. She glided towards the door by which she had entered. She glided from his sight.

Through the gray dawn she descended the great stairs, and passed through the deserted streets.— Back to the Hospital.— To do—not to think !

She entered the halls. She paced through them, feverishly searching for some sufferer who claimed constant, unremitting care.

She paused beside a bed. A nun stood laying wet cloths upon a child's head.

" Sister, let me take your place," said Lilian.

The nun looked up gratefully.

"How kind you are! It is not your hour for rising. But it is true that I am very tired," and she sat down and sighed wearily. "They must be changed every five minutes. It is his only chance, the doctor says." And she retreated.

Lilian stood ceaselessly renewing the cooling bandages, instinctively clinging to the compelled attention, the incessant occupation, as an anchor to her thoughts. Sharp, lancinating stabs seemed piercing her, red-hot irons searing her. It was Mira that she had tended through the night! Mira! A storm shook her at the name. She spoke it. "Mira." It sounded like the trumpet of death. Still she fulfilled her task.

Mr. Clinton stood ever before her, — his white face, his anguished look. How, how could she bear it. Might she not pray to die? All the passion, all the vehemence of her nature broke forth within her. The very foundations of her soul seemed yielding in that fearful strife. Still she fulfilled her task.

A nun entered the hall and approached her.

"Sister, the lady you watched last night begs that you will come again this evening."

"Say that I cannot come," said Lilian in a hoarse changed voice.

The nun withdrew.

Time passed. Still the storm raged in Lilian's breast, still the anguish hid from her all save its own immensity.

A nun came towards her.

" Sister, you are wanted in the reception-room."

As Lilian entered the room, a stranger met her eye.

" I come, my sister, to urge upon you the necessity of acceding to the wishes of the lady you tended last night. She is in a most critical state. Any excitement might destroy her at once. Whether she recovers or not depends principally upon her being kept entirely tranquil. She says that your voice reminds her of a dear friend, that your presence soothes and comforts her. She wept as she begged me to entreat you to come to-night, and I must tell you I think her life probably depends upon your granting her request.

Lilian stood grasping firmly the back of a chair. She closed her eyes as the physician ended, and turned her head away. For a while she stood motionless. Then she turned her face towards the stranger. It was ghastly pale.

" I will come," she said.

LXXI.

The evening was sinking into night, as again Lilian entered the high, richly-draped, shadowy room. As she approached the curtained bed, Mira took her hand and feebly pressed it.

" I am so glad that you are come."

She lay quite still for a while, apparently contented with the touch of Lilian's hand, then rousing herself, —

" Will you please to bring the lamp nearer," she said. " Your voice is so like hers, I want to see if you look like her."

Tremblingly Lilian obeyed.

She stood holding the lamp. Its light fell on her pale face, framed by the white bands and black veil, the eyes deepened with pain, the lips parting with apprehension, and on Mira's ethereal countenance, surrounded by masses of golden hair, the large, blue eyes looking into Lilian's with a longing, wistful gaze.

" When she is older she will look like you, but I hope she will never look so sad. I cannot bear to think of sorrow, coming to Lilian, my Lilian. Oh, if she were but with me now ! " And large tears rolled from Mira's eyes, as she still looked upwards into Lilian's face.

Lilian bent and kissed her forehead, choking down the gasping sobs which strove convulsively to break forth.

Mira's eyes closed, but still the tears fell slowly from between the golden lashes.

Suddenly a spasm contracted her frame. She looked affrightedly at Lilian. "It is coming," she exclaimed in a horror-stricken cry. "The crash,— Ah."— And she clung round Lilian's neck. "Hold me, hold me fast,— don't let me drown!" And she shook convulsively.

Lilian clasped her close.

"Do not be frightened. You are here, safe,— safe in my arms."

As the spasm passed, Mira pressed her hands to her forehead and moaned,—

"Oh that sound of rushing water,— will it never be stilled!— I have heard it so long.— I am so weary, so weary."

Lilian knelt beside her and drew her head upon her bosom.

"Rest here," she said.

Mira lay clasping Lilian's hand, her head pillowed upon her breast, quietly for a while, then she grew restless.

"Oh if I could only understand, if I could

only remember. Perhaps if I try to tell it, it
will help my thoughts. We were close by the
Bay of Naples. The night was cloudy. It was
so close that I could not sleep. My husband had
my mattress laid on the deck and sat down by
me. I fell asleep; and after that I can remember nothing, save the sound of rushing water and
a grinding crash, always coming back, till I found
myself in a room with my husband and an old
gray-headed physician. They told me I had
been very ill, and begged me not to ask any
questions. My husband was so altered, so careworn! All things seemed so different from what
they had been before! And when I looked in
the glass I did not know myself, I was so changed.
And I feel so tired I cannot think. I cannot remember. I cannot talk. If it were God's will
I should be glad to sleep, sleep here in your arms,
and never wake again. But I long to see Lilian
once more before I die. I know nothing about
her now, but I am sure that she loves me."

"Be sure that she loves you," burst from Lilian's lips as she pressed her cheek to the burning,
pulsing brow. "But pray do not talk. Your
fever is growing higher each moment."

"Yes, it is burning me up; but I like to talk

to you, and my thoughts are steadier to-night. I feel as if the clouds were opening. I can remember so much more clearly. I can recall all things as they were; the library with its cool shadows, Harvey writing, Lilian reading, while I sat busy at my work; and then the evenings when I used to sing.—They loved to hear me sing.—I sang every night. I loved best to sing this song," and she raised her voice, feeble but sweet and pure as in former days in the Litany, " Ruhn in Frieden alle Seelen."

Lilian sank on her knees and sobbed aloud, all possibility of self-control swept away.

The maid hastily appeared at the open door, then rang hurriedly.

" Send for Dr. Albertazzi and the other physician immediately."

" Oh ma'am, you will kill yourself. For God's sake don't sing."

Mira paid no heed. Her eyes were filled with strange light. Her voice grew fuller and clearer.

"What shall I do!" exclaimed the maid. "Dr. Albertazzi told me on no account whatever to call my master.

Lilian rose and leaned over Mira. She spoke to her. Mira gave no heed. Still she sang,

“Ruhn in Frieden.” Lilian wrung her hands. No sight, no sound without could reach Mira’s sense, again so suddenly darkened.

A rapid step passed through the antechamber. Dr. Albertazzi entered the room and advanced to where Mira lay. He questioned the maid.

“ I don’t know, Sir. The nun was with her.” Lilian came to his side.

“ You were sent for last night without my knowledge,” he said in a low voice; then louder, “ How has the night passed ? ”

“ She was quiet at first, then was seized with sudden terror. When that ceased, she began to talk of long-past scenes. I tried to quiet her in vain, still she talked, then she began to sing. She has sung ever since.” Lilian was trembling from head to foot.

The physician made no remark. He felt Mira’s pulse, laid his hand upon her head. Still the clear voice rang through the room, “ Ruhn in Frieden.”

“ Shall I not call Mr. Clinton, Sir ? ” asked the maid.

“ On no account,” he answered sternly.

The physician whom Lilian had seen that morning, entered. The two withdrew to a window and held a whispered consultation. The sound of their murmuring voices mixed with the song.·

As they left the window, Lilian drew near and looked into their faces.

"·We must wait until the excitement wears itself out. It is what we feared. There is nothing to be done."

They stood around the bed, and watched her, lying there, the chant of unearthly sweetness pouring from her unconscious lips. They watched long in solemn silence. At length the voice began imperceptibly to sink. Lower and lower. It murmured once more " Ruhn in Frieden," — and was still.

The physicians bent over her. She slept. Again they stood around the bed and watched. She slept.

The dawn began to break. The maid drew back the curtains and let in the faint light of day. As the light grew clearer, a change mysterious, awful, came over the sleeper's face. It grew thin and sharp. Mira opened her eyes, — large, bright, supernaturally searching. She looked around. Her breath came harshly. Her breast labored.

Dr. Albertazzi whispered to the maid. She left the room.

Mira's look rested on Lilian. It began to dim. She spoke.

"It grows dark. I am cold."

Lilian threw herself beside her. She clasped her in her arms. She pressed her lips to hers.

"Mira, Mira, do you not know me — do you not know Lilian ! — Oh God, save her, spare her, do not let her die ! "

As the victorious, self-immolating prayer broke from Lilian's lips, Mr. Clinton stood beside the bed.

A long, deep sigh breathed forth upon the awed stillness of the room. Another, — faint, — fainter, — it ceased.

Mira lay dead in Lilian's arms.

———◆———

LXXII.

THE registry of a foreign Protestant chapel bears this record : —

" Married, — Harvey Clinton to Lilian De-Kahn."

THE END.